Everybody else got excited when the first green shoots came up through the cold ground and the air lost its bite, but I'd start worrying about the summer. That bottomless hole in my year. No way to avoid it; I would stumble and begin falling, slowly, end over end, for two months that went on forever, waiting to crash back into the autumn again, like a bad dream that wakes you up in the middle of the night covered by sweat, with a cold lump in your stomach.

But this summer was spinning along. . . .

ONE FAT SUMMER

Robert Lipsyte

📚 **HarperTrophy®**
An Imprint of HarperCollins*Publishers*

One Fat Summer

Copyright © 1977 by Robert M. Lipsyte

Library of Congress Cataloging-in-Publication Data
Lipsyte, Robert.
One fat summer.
Summary: An overweight fourteen-year-old boy experiences a
turning-point summer in which he learns to stand up for himself.
ISBN 0-06-447073-3 (pbk.)
[1. Weight control—Fiction.] I. Title.
PZ7.L67On   76-49746
[Fic]   CIP
                                                                    AC

3 1350 00314 7925

First Harper Trophy editon, 1991
Revised Harper Trophy edition, 2004
Visit us on the World Wide Web!
www.harperteen.com

11 12 13 OPM 40 39 38 37 36 35 34

For Sam and Susannah

1

I always hated summertime. When people take off their clothes. In winter you can hide yourself. Long coats, heavy jackets, thick sweaters. Nobody can tell how fat you really are. But in the summertime they can see your thick legs and your wobbly backside and your big belly and your soft arms. And they laugh.

I never would have gone to the Rumson Lake Community Association Carnival on the Fourth of July if it hadn't been cool enough that night to wear a long-sleeved knit shirt outside my pants. At the start of that summer, my fourteenth, I couldn't button the waist of any of my pants without getting a stomachache. I weighed more than 200 pounds on July 4th. I don't know exactly how much more because I jumped off the bathroom scale when the number 200 rolled up. The numbers were still climbing past the pointer when I bailed out.

I was tall for my age and I had large, heavy bones, so I didn't look like a circus freak. Just like a very fat boy. When my pants weren't strangling my belly, and if there were no scales or mirrors around, I could forget for a while that I was fat. But sooner or later there'd be someone around to remind me. The wise guys started up as soon as we got to the carnival, at Marino's Beach Club and Snack Bar.

"Hey, it's the Crisco Kid," yelled one of the older teenagers hanging around the snack bar.

"Why do you call him the Crisco Kid?" It sounded like a comedy routine. I knew what was coming.

"Because he's fat in the can."

They all laughed. My face got hot, but I pretended I hadn't heard. Rule number one: never let people know they can get to you or they'll never stop trying. Joanie pretended she hadn't heard, either.

"Look at that girl he's with. The nose knows."

"She's the one who blew the wind in."

I felt embarrassed for Joanie. Someday I'd wake up thin, I believed that. But poor Joanie was stuck with that nose for her whole life. It was long and crooked. The rest of her face was pretty, but who ever looked at the rest of her face?

"Hey, let's go to the booths," she said. "I feel lucky tonight." Joanie was a terrific pretender, too.

It was early, there was still light in the sky, and the crowds hadn't arrived yet. Strings of colored bulbs danced in the breeze off the lake. The jukebox was playing "Little White Cloud That Cried."

"There's that dumb song again," I said.

"It's not so bad when you're in the mood," said Joanie.

"I'm only in the mood when I've got an umbrella."

"That's a joke, son," said Joanie. "It was only funny the first twenty-seven times you said it."

"Then how come you never laughed?"

"Ha-ha. Okay?"

Then we both laughed.

I've known Joanie since we were three years old. Our parents were best friends. In the city we lived in the same apartment house and we were always in the same classes in school. Somewhere there's a picture of us taking a bath together when we were four. It's cute. I wasn't so fat then, and her nose wasn't so huge. Joanie and I not only grew up together, we grew *out* together. That's my joke, but I've never told it to her.

A few years ago, when my parents bought a summer house on Rumson Lake, her parents bought one, too. And after that we were together summer and winter. She taught me to dance, but I never danced with anyone except her. We did our homework together. When her father took her mother on a business trip, Joanie stayed at my house.

Joanie and I talked about almost everything; she was a great talker, but only with me. Otherwise she was shy. The only things in the world we didn't talk about were her nose and my fat. When we were alone together I felt thin, and I think she felt pretty. I guess that's why we were such good friends.

"Step right up, ladies and gentlemen, the

wheel of fortune is spinning, spinning, spinning. For one thin dime you can win a beautiful doll to call your own.'' It was Pete Marino himself, as usual dressed in nothing except a little bathing suit and a St. Christopher medal around his neck. He was pointing at us. ''Now here's a couple of gamblers. Step right up, folks, you look lucky to me.''

''Let's go try the ringtoss,'' I said. Muscles like Pete Marino's gave me a stomachache. Cannonball muscles with big blue veins over them. I didn't have any muscles, and my veins were buried in fat.

Joanie slapped a dime on number fourteen.

''I thought six was your lucky number.''

''Not anymore. My age is my lucky number now.''

''Round and round it goes, where it stops nobody knows,'' chanted Pete Marino. He was waving his arms at the wheel and doing a little dance. He must have known how all the muscles on his back twitched and jumped under his smooth bronze skin.

''He's not conceited,'' I said. ''He's convinced.''

''C'mon, he's very nice,'' said Joanie. But

then she looked at me. "He's not as smart as you, though."

"The wheel is slowing down, soon we'll have a winner. Who's it gonna be?" He turned around, grinning. He had big white teeth, like Chiclets, and curly golden hair. He looked like a movie star. "Who'll be the lucky one?"

Joanie's dime was the only one on the counter. A few people drifted over to watch. The wheel stopped on fourteen. Joanie started to scream, then put her hands over her mouth.

"A winner!" Pete Marino looked happier than she did. "The first winner of the evening." He waved at a row of stuffed animals. "Take your pick, sweetheart."

Joanie picked an enormous pink teddy bear. Pete made a big deal of getting it down and presenting it to her.

"Do we have to lug that around all night?" I asked. "Can't we leave it here and pick it up later?"

"You don't have to carry it," said Joanie.

"Hey, folks, you can bring it back a little later and I'll hold it for you," said Pete, "but it would help business if you walk around with it for a little while. All proceeds go to the community association, you know.''

"Sure," said Joanie.

"Thanks, honey." He gave her a big, sexy wink. What did he have to do that for? He's eighteen years old, maybe nineteen, a sophomore in college. On a swimming scholarship, of course.

"Hey, big fella." He gave me the same wink exactly. "Take care of that little lady, you've got a real winner there."

Actually, I knew he was a nice guy. He wouldn't remember it, but he talked to me a couple of years ago. The summer the Marino family opened the Beach Club, Pete gave some free swimming lessons, and I went a few times. He told me I had the makings of a really good swimmer, and I should stick with it. But I started feeling embarrassed in a bathing suit about then, and I never did.

Joanie and I strolled along the beach where the booths were set up. People stared at the big pink teddy bear. Usually I hate it when people stare at me, but this was kind of fun.

"You know," I said to Joanie, "we have to

get going on our project. We don't even have an idea yet.''

"We'll think of something," she said.

She didn't seem too enthusiastic, but you couldn't be sure about Joanie. She didn't like anyone, even me, to know what was going on inside her. She tried to keep the same expression on her face whether she was happy or sad. And she was sarcastic a lot to cover up. You had to understand her.

We walked around for awhile and tried a few more booths. Ringtoss, the baseball throw, a different wheel of fortune. Nothing. I steered her away from the shooting gallery because the greasy punks from the snack bar were hanging out there now, cheering for a tall, skinny guy in brown combat boots and a Marine fatigue hat, who was puncturing the balloons with a BB rifle faster than Pete's older brother, Vinnie, could blow them up. What a marksman.

The jukebox played "Any Time" by Eddie Fisher, and a few couples began dancing on the wooden dock where the rowboats and canoes were tied up. People were pouring in. From a distance I saw my parents and Joanie's parents come in together. A few guys turned to look at a really built girl with long black hair. She was wearing a Barnard College sweatshirt and red shorts. One of the guys whistled, but she ignored him. Then I realized it was only my sister, Michelle.

There was a scream from Pete Marino's booth, and a woman began waving a black-and-white panda. Another winner.

"We can take the teddy bear back now," I said to Joanie.

"It's not so heavy." She was hugging it.

"You going to carry it around all night? Where you going to put it when we eat?"

"Bob?" Joanie was just about the only person who called me Bob. Usually it was Bobby or Robert or some other things. "We won't be able to start our project right away."

"Well, if you want to take a few days' vacation, that's okay. We've got all summer."

"I was going to call you tomorrow. We're going back to the city," she said.

"What for?"

"We have to go back."

"For how long?"

9

"I don't know. Maybe two weeks."

"How come?"

"We just have to, that's all." Her mouth snapped shut. Case closed. She'd be a great spy. You could torture her, if she didn't want to talk, forget it.

"Well, what am I supposed to do?"

"Stand on your head and spit nickels, how should I know?"

"Boy, you sure took your nasty pills this morning. I was counting on doing this project. You said in the city you'd do it, we told the teacher." I felt my summer plans crumbling under me. I had figured the project, an extra-credit paper for economics or civics about local businesses or government, would keep my father off my back till Labor Day.

"You could start it without me," she said.

"Oh, boy, this is really going to mess things up for me."

"Well, I'm coming back. It's only a couple of weeks, you said we had the whole summer."

"But you don't understand. He's not going to let me hang around for a couple of weeks."

"Your father?"

"I had to talk myself blue in the face about the project; I even told him that the teacher *assigned* it to us, that if we didn't do it we wouldn't get into the Honor Society."

"Why'd you tell him that?"

"He wants me to go to day camp."

"You're too old for day camp."

"As a junior counselor. You still have to pay, but they let you help out with the little kids. Big deal."

"He didn't make you go last year."

"Yeah, but he's going to be in the city most of the summer, just coming up on weekends, and Michelle's working at camp, and my mother's going to be busy every day studying to be a teacher. He says I have to be doing something."

"Which camp?"

"He gave me a big choice. Mohawk Hill or Happy Valley."

"Some choice."

"The pit or the pendulum. What's so important in the city?"

"Maybe you could be a junior counselor for a couple of weeks," she said.

"I don't want to go to camp for a minute.

Besides, you have to pay for the whole summer in advance. You know my father, once he pays for something, that's it. Remember the pickled beets?''

"I can still taste them." That got a little smile out of her.

I could still taste them too. It seemed like we ate them every meal for the whole winter. My father thought he was getting five cases of different vegetables, but they were all beets. And when he couldn't get his money back, we just had to eat them all up.

"I'll tell you a secret about those beets," I lowered my voice. "That whole winter, my pee was red."

"Oh, Bob." She laughed. I felt a little better.

"Can't you do anything? You could stay at my house while your folks are in the city. You could sleep in Michelle's room, she wouldn't mind. Or you could have my room and I'll sleep on the couch."

"No, I have to go, too."

"What are you going to do there?"

"Curiosity killed the cat," she said.

"But satisfaction brought him back."

"Well, why don't you start the project?"

"That wouldn't be any fun," I said. "Besides, he'd never go for that. He'd think I'd just fool around if you weren't doing it, too. He doesn't have much confidence in me."

"Maybe you could get a job for a couple of weeks."

"Oh, sure."

"There are always ads for jobs on the bulletin board by the snack bar."

"To watch little kids at the beach."

"So what's wrong with that for a couple of weeks? At least it would keep you out of camp."

I couldn't answer that truthfully, even to Joanie. It would be as bad as camp. You've got to wear a bathing suit and go in the water, or at least shorts and a T-shirt. It's bad enough when older kids call you fatso. When five-year-olds do it . . .

"I hate little kids," I said.

"How about cutting lawns?" she asked.

"Who would hire me?"

"You could lie about your age. You do look older."

"You need junior working papers. Your age is right on the papers."

13

"You don't need them to cut lawns. C'mon, let's see what's on the bulletin board."

"Let's eat first."

"Right now?"

"Skip it. I'll figure something out," I said.

"Nothing doing, you made the big deal about me letting you down. . . ."

"I never said that."

"You thought that."

"What are you, a mind reader or something?"

"Yep. C'mon. Move." Joanie was tough. I'm really tougher, but I let her lead me to the snack bar because I knew she felt bad about letting me down.

"Hey." The punks were back. "What time does the balloon go up?"

"Think you could hit that balloon, Willie?"

Willie, the tall skinny marksman, took a pack of Lucky Strikes out of his fatigue hat and shook out a cigarette. "He looks more like a beach ball to me." He wore his blond hair in a duck's ass, high on top, long and pointy in the back.

Joanie was at the bulletin board. "Here's one. 'Boy wanted to maintain large estate. One dollar an hour. Call RU-9-4849.' "

14

"I'll call tomorrow. From home."

"Call now."

"I don't have a nickel."

"Here." She handed me a nickel.

"After we eat."

"You want me to dial for you?"

Willie strolled over. He snapped open a Zippo and lit his cigarette. "You sure your fingers'll fit into the dial?" The hoody-looking boys and girls behind him snickered.

"Let's go," I whispered to Joanie.

"Call now," she said out loud.

"Call now," mimicked Willie.

Joanie whirled on him. "Why don't you crawl back into your hole."

"Don't point that nose at me. It might be loaded." His gang laughed.

"Hey, folks." Pete Marino walked up. Willie took a step backward. "Did you want to leave that bear while you're eating?"

"It's all right." Joanie was hugging it very tightly.

"She needs it, it's her date," said Willie.

Pete Marino never stopped smiling. "Take a hike, Rummie."

"It's a free country," said Willie. He blew a smoke ring. "And I fought for it, college boy."

Pete didn't say a word. But his muscles seemed to swell and the long blue veins down his arms stood out.

"Willie?" One of the girls touched his arm. "Let's ride over to Lenape Falls. This place is dead."

Willie took his time finishing his cigarette. He flicked the butt at the ground near my feet. Joanie and I watched them swagger to the parking lot and pile into a souped-up blue-and-white Chevrolet. Willie gunned the car onto the county road. Long after we couldn't see it anymore, we heard it roaring into the night.

Pete was gone. My legs felt weak.

"No more excuses," said Joanie. "Call."

I had no energy to argue with her. A man's voice answered on the second ring. "Dr. Kahn speaking. Yes?"

"I'm calling about the lawn job. I saw your sign on the bulletin board at the snack bar."

"Are you experienced?"

"Experienced?" I looked at Joanie. She nodded her head furiously. "Yes."

"Come over Sunday afternoon and we'll talk. Do you know where I am?"

"No."

"At the north end of Rumson Lake, toward Lenape Falls. My name's on the mailbox. What's your name?"

"Robert Marks."

He hung up.

"Well?"

I was casual. "Sunday afternoon I'm going for an interview."

"See?"

"That doesn't mean I'll get the job."

"He hardly asked anything about you. He must be desperate for someone to cut his lawn. He'll hire anybody."

"Thanks a million."

"You know what I mean." She hit my arm with the teddy bear's leg. That was very affectionate for Joanie. "Now we can go eat."

We ran into her parents on the way to the hot dog stand. They seemed nervous and anxious to leave, and they wanted her to go home with them. Usually Joanie puts up a fight, and usually she gets her way, but this time her mother

17

whispered something in her ear, and Joanie just nodded and followed them out. She asked me to stop by Sunday and tell her if I got the job.

I ate about five hot dogs and drank two cream sodas before my sister caught me. Michelle's always needling me to lose weight. She started up again, but when the loudspeaker blared an announcement for Pete Marino's diving exhibition we followed the crowd to the dock. We watched him climb slowly to the top of the platform and step out on the twenty-foot highboard. I got a stomachache just seeing someone up that high. He smiled and waved.

"He's not conceited," said Michelle. "He's convinced."

"He's a nice guy," I said.

"How would you know?"

"I know."

"You never even talked to him."

"That's what you think." Usually when I say that she makes a face and walks away. Not this time.

"Prove it," she said.

"Prove I don't. You're going to college next year, you know all the answers."

She sighed. "I guess you will be a writer when you grow up. If you ever grow up. You're such a liar already."

"Okay, big mouth, listen to this." I told her how Pete moved in so cool and easy when Willie and his gang were giving us a hard time. I made a few changes here and there, nothing too important. I didn't mention the phone call to Dr. Kahn, and I made it seem as if Pete and I had stood side by side to face down the gang.

"We should thank him," said Michelle. She thinks she's got such smooth moves, but she never fools me, not for a minute.

"He's just dying to meet you. He asked me who was that girl wearing the *Ber*-nard shirt, and I said it was the name of your steady boyfriend."

"You're funny like a crutch."

"Take a hike, big mouth. And don't use me to get yourself a date." I didn't say it loud enough for her to catch every single word.

She made a face and walked away. I found my parents, and we watched Pete dive a few times. He was merely great. They said they were going home. I didn't feel like walking up our hill, so I rode back with them. They were arguing about something, but I wasn't listening. I was thinking about the job, and about the way Pete handled Willie. Let Michelle thank him if she wanted to. It was dumb. Thanking him would be like thanking the Lone Ranger.

2

The first time I ever saw Dr. Kahn's lawn it looked like a velvet sea, a green velvet sea that flowed up from the gray shore of the county road to surround a great white house with white columns. The house looked like a proud clipper ship riding the crest of the ocean. As I trudged up from the county road I made out the figure of a man standing on the front porch, the captain on the bridge of his ship. As I got closer, I saw he was rocking an old-fashioned baby carriage. I could hear children yelling from somewhere behind the house, and the laughter of grown-ups.

When I got to the porch I had to stand still and take deep breaths. My knees were quivering and my stomach boiling. My face was on fire. My tongue was swollen and dry.

The man just stared at me. His eyes were black and deep and set close together, like shotgun barrels. His lips were so thin his mouth looked like a slit for old razor blades. Finally, he spoke.

"You're the boy who called about the lawn job."

"Yek." My mouth was so dry it was the best I could do.

He stopped rocking the carriage and leaned forward. He was wearing a white shirt without a tie, black pants and red-leather slippers.

"What's your name?"

"Robert Marks."

"Where do you live?"

"Across the lake."

"How did you get here?"

"I walked."

"On such a hot day. That shows enterprise. I like a boy with enterprise. Are you an all-year-rounder?"

"I'm from the city. We come up summers."

"How old are you?"

I had carefully rehearsed this answer. "Feverteen," I mumbled.

"Speak up, speak up."

I swallowed and lied. "Seventeen."

The baby in the carriage began to cry and Dr. Kahn started rocking it again. I felt seasick. "You will receive seventy-five cents an hour. Dr. Kahn pays top dollar. But you'll work for it. Oh, you'll work for it."

A little girl in a blue playsuit ran past the porch chasing a rolling ball. She waved at Dr. Kahn and he waved back.

"You'll make this place look beautiful for the weekends. You'll cut the lawn, trim the hedges, rake the gravel, weed the rock garden. You'll wash the car, mop the pool deck, clean the garbage pails. And whatever else needs to be done." His eyes snapped shut and open like window shades. "Of course, I have a gardening service come on Fridays for the skilled work. Any questions?"

"No, sir."

"You'll be here at nine o'clock sharp every weekday morning, beginning tomorrow. You'll bring your own lunch. You'll work until three o'clock sharp in the afternoon. Understand?"

"Yes, sir."

23

"I will see you here tomorrow at nine A.M. Sharp." The shotgun eyes became deeper, blacker, closer. "How old did you say you were?"

This time I didn't have to lie. "I said I was seventeen."

He began nodding his head in rhythm to the rocking. "You are extremely fat for seventeen."

Then he turned his back on me and looked into the carriage.

I floated down the gravel driveway. If I had any breath to spare I would have sung as I walked on the shoulder of the county road that circles the lake. I was going to stop off at Joanie's house to tell her the good news but something happened that made me forget. A car pulled up alongside me, a souped-up blue-and-white Chevrolet with a row of cherries painted on the door.

"Hey. You. Got a license?"

"Me?"

"I asked you if you had a license, fats." The car was packed with laughing faces, but the only thing I could see clearly was a long thin arm hanging out of the driver's window. It was tattooed with a Marine Corps insignia and the name Willie.

"A license?"

"Yeah, for that trailer you're hauling behind you."

The car rocked with laughter. Willie poked out his pointed rat face. "Listen, fats, if I catch you around the lake again without a license for that big can of yours, I'll run you right back to the city where you belong."

The car screeched off, and my nose and mouth were filled with the stink of burning rubber.

3

At breakfast my father asked, "Well, Robert, have you made up your mind?"

"Not yet." I drank my orange juice in two swallows. It's the only way to drink cold, fresh-squeezed orange juice. You fill your mouth with it to wash away all the cotton from sleep, then gulp it down, feel it rush down your pipes and splash into your stomach, whoosh. It also drives my father up the wall, and I was hoping he'd start giving me the usual lesson in table manners and forget the cross-examination. No such luck.

"When do you plan to reach a decision?"

"Soon."

"That's not soon enough."

"What's soon enough?" I asked.

"You'll get shut out of everything if you don't

26

step on it." He was making a big show of being patient. But his muscles were popping along his jaw. My father's thin, but he's got muscles and veins everywhere. "You'll have nothing to do all summer. No camp, no swim classes, nothing. You'll have nothing to do but hang around and feel sorry for yourself. And eat."

"Hot stuff," said my mother, bringing plates of bacon and scrambled eggs to the table. Great timing.

"Where's Michelle?" snapped my father.

"Here's Michelle," said Michelle. Her face was still swollen from sleep. She was rubbing her eyes. I wondered what time she came home from her counselors' meeting last night.

"This isn't a restaurant," said my father.

"I'm glad to hear that," said my mother.

I started to eat. There's really only one way to eat scrambled eggs, bacon and toast, and this is the way: First, you shovel a heaping forkful of eggs into your mouth, feel the butter run inside your gums, press the soft little clumps of egg against the roof of your mouth with your tongue, then poke in a crispy, crackly bacon stick, chew until the bacon is scattered through the mouthful of eggs, then jam in a bite of crunchy toast, and chew slowly, making sure your lips are closed so nothing leaks out. Soft and hard, buttery and burnt, all pressing against the inside of your cheeks. A full mouth. And it's only the first.

It's even better when your father isn't staring at you in disgust.

"Robert. I don't think you're taking this seriously."

"Yesum."

"Don't talk with your mouth full."

I had to swallow ahead of schedule. "Why do I have to make plans all the time? I'm on vacation."

"A man has to do something with his life. The sooner you start the better."

"Let him finish his breakfast, Marty," said my mother.

"Well, Robert?" asked my father.

"Maybe I'll get a job," I said.

He snorted. "Be serious."

If I had any thought of telling him about Dr. Kahn, I cancelled it right then. Even if he let me do it, what a big deal. Robert, you will wear steel-tipped shoes so you don't cut off your clumsy toes, and goggles for your eyes and heavy gloves for your fat little fingers. A helmet! Perhaps a complete set of armor. And I'd clank off to work, and get fired, and everybody would feel sorry for me, and be really nice. Poor Bobby, cut from the team again. I'd been through it all before. He didn't have much confidence in me.

"Personally," said my father, "and it's all your decision, I lean toward Mohawk Hill. There seems to be more physical activity there, and they don't have ice cream in the afternoon."

"Marty, his eggs are getting cold, let him eat."

"It's for his own good, Lenore. He's not going to thank you ten years from now when he weighs three hundred pounds."

Michelle jumped up. "Hey. I'm going to be late, I'm going to miss my bus." She kissed my father's cheek. "Have a good week. See you Friday night."

I silently thanked her for changing the subject, but then she said, "Keep your chins up, Bobby." She charged out.

"I better get going, too," said my father. He

stood up. "Get on the stick, Robert." He mussed my hair. He went back to his room to finish dressing.

My mother said, "Ride into town with me. I'm going to do some shopping, we can have lunch out."

"No, thanks, I think I'll walk around the lake, maybe stop off at Joanie's."

"I'll drop you."

"I'd like the exercise."

"You'll watch the traffic, Bobby."

"That's what I'll do this summer. Watch the traffic."

"Lenore!"

"Coming. Bobby, I'll see you later. We'll figure something out together."

She kissed me and hurried out to the driveway. My father was already on his way to the car. They always had a big good-bye scene at the railroad station. You'd think he was going off to war. Big deal. Five days sitting behind a desk in an air-conditioned office. He probably goes to the movies every night. And eats in restaurants where he can order anything he wants. Of course he never gains a pound. In his life, I'm sure he never held his breath while buttoning his shirt. Or had to wear his shirt outside his pants because the zipper wouldn't come all the way up.

I finished breakfast and cleared the table. My Monday-morning chore. Then I packed myself a lunch, a couple of salami sandwiches, an orange, an apple, a few cookies, nothing too heavy, and got dressed in sneakers, a long-sleeved shirt and dungarees that almost fit.

Be serious, huh? A man has to do something with his life, huh? Betcha I work harder today than you do, Dad.

4

Rumson Lake is round with an island in the middle. The island has trees and an abandoned wooden shack. I'd never been on the island, but a lot of couples went there at night to make out. At night you could see the light of campfires. When there's a full moon, you could see canoes and rowboats bobbing along the shore of the island.

This morning the only action around the island was Vinnie and Pete Marino swimming their laps. Each of them had a red inner tube jerking along behind, tied to an ankle by rope. In case of a cramp, all they'd have to do is grab the tube and paddle in. Even great swimmers can get a cramp and drown.

The Marinos became great swimmers because

their oldest sister, Connie, got polio one summer. She spent months in the hospital, and when she went home she had to wear a brace on one leg. The doctors said she would never walk normally again. Mrs. Marino prayed for her recovery every single morning, in church. Then one day Mr. Marino, a big tough guy who owns a cement company in the city, went to church and told God that all he wanted out of life was to dance with Connie at her wedding, and if God did that for him then God could do anything he wanted with him.

I heard this story from my parents who heard it from Mr. Marino at a Community Association meeting.

Well, Mr. Marino heard a voice telling him to take Connie to the waters. Mrs. Marino thought it meant some place with holy waters, like Lourdes, but Mr. Marino said it meant Rumson Lake. And for the whole next summer every member of the family took turns holding Connie in the water; and first she could only float, and then she could kick her bad leg a little, and by the end of that summer she was swimming. The next summer she was walking by herself, and now she hardly has a limp at all. That was ten years ago.

Because of all that swimming, everybody got to be pretty good. Vinnie was the star of his high school team, and Pete was the city butterfly champion. There's another brother coming up who's supposed to be the best of them all. If I do become a writer someday, that'll make a good story for the *Reader's Digest*.

I watched the Marinos for a minute. They glided through the water like sharks, fast and steady, their arms cutting the water with every little splash. A light breeze stirred the water, and the morning sun glistened on the small, silvery waves.

I felt really good striding around the lake on the county road. The breeze was in my face, and I swung my arms in rhythm with my legs. A couple of times I waved to truck drivers. They always waved back. Someday I might drive a truck, a big one, with my sleeves rolled up to my shoulders and a baseball cap pulled down over my eyes. Truck drivers have adventures. Jack Smith, who used to drive a laundry truck, once jumped out of his rig, ran into a burning house and saved a baby. When he got back to the garage the foreman started yelling at him for coming late. The way I heard the story from Joanie, Jack just stared at the foreman; he never said a word about what had happened, just sucked on his cigarette like Humphrey Bogart until the foreman was finished yelling. Then he threw his cigarette on the ground, rubbed it out with the toe of his boot, and knocked out the foreman with one punch. What a man! The boss was watching and fired Jack on the spot. Jack just turned and walked away. The next morning, when the boss read in the newspaper what Jack had done, he drove to the trailer where he lived and offered him his old job back, with a big raise. Jack told him what he could do with his job. I heard somewhere that Jack Smith has his own business now. I've got that story filed in the back of my mind, too. It would make a good short story for *The Saturday Evening Post*.

I reached Dr. Kahn's lawn at exactly 8:47 by my wristwatch. It was probably 8:48. My watch always runs a minute slow because of my metabolism. That's the speed at which your body burns up energy. Once I took a test called a

Basal Metabolism. I lay in a doctor's office for an hour breathing into a rubber mouthpiece connected by a tube to a machine. My nose was clipped shut. Afterward, the doctor said I had a low normal Basal Metabolism, which means my body burns up food a little slower than most other bodies. That's why I put on weight easily. The doctor made a joke about it. He said I could walk into a bakery, and if I took too deep a breath, I'd gain a pound. My father and Michelle have high Basal Metabolisms, which means they could eat a pound of cake and burn it right off. That's why they're always bothering me about my weight, they don't understand the problem. My mother is a normal Basal Metabolism, so she sort of understands. The doctor told her that I'd probably start losing weight sometime in my teens, so she doesn't make such a big fuss about it. She's had a few arguments with my father about my weight. She thinks he needles me about it too much. I think my father's sort of ashamed of having a fat son. He wants me to be lean and athletic like he is.

I made it up Dr. Kahn's gravel driveway in under nine minutes. 8:57 A.M.

He was waiting for me on the porch steps and looking at his watch.

"Two minutes late," he said. He must be a high Basal. "I don't like tardiness in a boy. See that it doesn't happen again. You'll work until 3:02 P.M."

"Yes, sir." No point making a federal case on my first day. I hadn't saved a baby or anything.

"Follow me."

We walked around the back of the house past a swimming pool. The place was deserted. We walked into a toolshed that was as big as some of the cottages around the lake. It was dark and cool in the shed. Hanging from the walls, in neat rows, were rakes, shovels, hoes, pitchforks, clean and shining in the dim light. I couldn't wait to get my hands on them. My father never let me use his garden tools, he thought I would break them or leave them out in the rain to get rusty. Just give me a good shovel and I'll make the dirt fly. I felt excited. Dr. Kahn pointed toward a green motorized lawn mower. I had never worked a power mower before. At home we had a hand mower. It was rusty from all the nights I left it out.

"You know how to operate this?"

"Sure."

"Pull it out."

I dragged the mower out of the shed. It was much heavier than it looked.

"Each morning, before you begin, you'll clean the blade, and check the gas and oil." He untied a length of rope from the handle, wrapped it around a cylinder on top of the motor, and yanked. The motor roared to life, the spinning blade sprayed grit.

"Watch for stones, they'll chip the blade. You'll be responsible for damage." He walked away.

I pushed the mower to the front of the house. He hadn't told me the direction in which I was supposed to mow—up and down the hill, the long way, or from side to side. My decision. My father was very fussy about my cutting in long rows. He hated it when I made designs or cut in squares, which he said wasted energy. I decided to cut from side to side, it made more sense than pushing the heavy mower all the way up the hill from the county road, then running down the hill after it.

Cutting the first few rows was uncomfortable until I got my fingers just right around the rubber handlebar grips and figured out the best distance between me and the mower. If I was too close my belly banged against the handlebars, which hurt, and I couldn't use my shoulders to push. If I was too far away I'd have to bend so far forward with my arms outstretched that my back ached.

And then I got the right grip and the right position, and it was easy. What a job! A piece of cake. Ho, boy, I can do this in my sleep, like the Marinos knocking off laps. If I could swim the way I cut lawns, I thought, I'd be the city champ, too. This lawn will win prizes. Just back and forth, nice and easy, follow the lines of the last cut, straight as an arrow, watch for stones. You old devil lawn, you don't have a chance against me and my green machine. I'm gonna cut you down to size, lawn.

Power surged out of my chest and shoulders, through my arms, out my fingers into the green machine. Scraps of grass flew out from under the mower. My nostrils twitched with the beautiful stinging smell of fresh-cut grass. I felt like singing. So I made up a song, and sang it.

Listen to the birds,
The eagles and the larks,
Saying good-bye, grass,
Here comes Big Bob Marks.

I felt terrific. What a great summer this is going to be. I've reached a decision, I've got a plan, don't worry about me hanging around all summer feeling sorry for myself. I've got a job. I got it all by myself, nobody helped me. Well, almost all by myself. Wait till they find out about it. They'll be proud. And they should be. Nobody ever cut a lawn like I'm cutting this lawn. By the time I'm finished with this lawn it'll look like a wall-to-wall carpet. Smooooth.

I've got a job. My own money. Seventy-five cents an hour, six hours a day, that's four dollars and fifty cents. Five days. That's twenty-two dollars and fifty cents a week. My own money. I'm rich. I won't tell anybody for a while. One day I'll go into town, buy some earrings for Mom, a belt for Dad; I might even get Michelle some perfume. I'll write a note with that: For a sister who smells. When they ask me where I got the money, I'll tell them I robbed a bank. A man has to do something with his life. I don't find that amusing, Robert. Now, Bobby, we really appreciate these presents, but . . .

And then I'll tell them. That'll get a smile out of my father. He'll be proud of me.

I'll get Joanie a book of poems. Emily Dickinson. She loves Emily Dickinson. I can't wait to tell her about my job. She'll have a lot to say about it.

Ouch. A small stone shot out from under the mower and bounced off my ankle. Watch those stones. I was just about to stop and rub my ankle, it really hurt, when I noticed that Dr. Kahn was watching me from the porch. Wouldn't want him to know I ran over a stone.

The sun was prickling the little hairs on the back of my neck. I could use one of those big white cavalry hats John Wayne wears in the movies. Captain Marks of the U.S. Cavalry, the only man who understands the Apaches. He grew up with them after his parents were killed in a wagon-train massacre. A renegade band has broken loose from the reservation, led by Chief Willie Ratface. They're on the warpath, raiding settlements; nobody's safe. And the colonel's daughter is coming in on the next stagecoach to visit our desolate desert outpost. Captain Marks and his rough-and-tumble troopers, the dregs of the cavalry who'll take orders only from him, will ride out and save her.

Once I had a U.S. Cavalry hat. I had a complete U.S. Cavalry uniform with a holster belt that went around your waist and over your shoulder, and a metal cap pistol shaped like a six-shooter. My grandparents sent it to me for my birthday. The pants were blue with a yellow stripe down the leg. The jacket was blue, too, and had captain's bars on the shoulders, and ribbons and shiny gold buttons. It was beautiful. But it didn't fit. Not even the hat.

I couldn't button the jacket or zipper the pants or even get the belt around my waist. I never even got to play with the gun because my mother wanted to keep the set new so she could exchange the uniform for a larger size. But it was the largest size they made. I guess I was around eight or nine years old then. My father wanted me to keep it, he said it would give me an incentive to lose weight so I could fit into it. I wished they had given it away. Just looking at that uniform in its box made me feel so bad I ate more. One day when I was alone in the house I opened a box of Hydrox cookies and jammed them into my mouth, fast as I could, not caring about the brown crumbs spilling out of the corners of my mouth; just jammed in those cookies faster than I could chew them, swallowing lumps of cookies big as Ping-Pong balls that got stuck in my throat and chest until I choked and had to wash them down with cold milk. They still hurt going down, I felt every Hydrox Ping-Pong ball push through my throat and chest until it fell with a thump into my stomach. And still I couldn't stop until I'd finished every cookie in the box, and then I had to lie down. My stomach had turned to concrete. I couldn't move for hours until it was digested.

I felt hungry. I looked at my watch. 9:42 A.M. That's all it was. I'd been cutting only a little more than a half hour. How could time move so slowly? The world must have a low Basal Metabolism today.

Keep cutting. Can't stop. He's watching me from the porch. My mouth got dry and my nose was filled with fumes from the gasoline engine, and every time I turned to start a new row, pain exploded in my wrists and shot up my arms into my shoulders. My fingers were numb, I'd never be able to pry them off the handlebar grips. My back hurt. My head hurt. My feet were very hot. I was sweating all over, even my knees and elbows were sweating. Each scorching drop of sweat rolled slowly down my chest and back like a scorching drop of acid burning out a furrow in my skin. If only I could take off my shirt like everybody else who cuts grass. But my pants weren't buttoned, and, anyway, I never take off my shirt when people are watching.

Everything was getting hazy. Trees swayed and there wasn't even a breeze. The lawn began to move. It rippled. Everything was wavy; it was like looking at the world through a fish tank. The lawn began to roll like the ocean. I was getting lawn sick.

And then the motor stopped. Just stopped dead. I hadn't realized how loud the mower was, how its roar banged against my ears and clogged my brain, until it was suddenly silent and I heard birds tweet again and crickets chirp and the whoosh of traffic on the county road. Far away, a dog barked.

Why did it stop? Did I break it? The sweat turned cold on my skin. I have to start it again. The rope was still on the handlebars. I tried to remember how Dr. Kahn had started the engine. Wind the rope around the cylinder, and pull. I had trouble opening my hands, they were locked into hooks around the grips.

Out of the corner of my eye I saw Dr. Kahn step off the porch and start down the lawn toward me. My hands slowly opened. They were red and swollen. I wrapped the rope around the cylinder, and pulled. The motor whined, and died. I tried again. This time, nothing.

I heard his slippers slapping against his heels. I pulled with all my might, lost my balance, and tripped over the mower. I could have just stayed there, sprawled out on the lawn, my face in the sweet grass. But he was coming and I jumped up.

"You're out of gas," he said. The shotgun eyes blasted right through me. He unscrewed a little cap on the side of the motor and stuck his finger in the gas tank. It came out dry. "A gas mower runs on gas. Did you know that?"

"Yek."

"The gas is in the shed. And don't forget the funnel."

The hill seemed steeper now, it was like climbing a mountain. A very steep, short mountain. I was much closer to the porch than I thought. I hadn't cut all that much grass.

I felt better in the shed, soothed by the coolness and the darkness. I found a gallon can of gasoline and a funnel. Outside again, the heat slammed into me like a wall of hot wet cotton. My tongue stuck to the roof of my mouth, and I could hardly breathe.

"Is this job too tough for you?" Dr. Kahn had followed me up.

"Nnnnnnn . . ." It was the best my stuck tongue could do.

"What was that?"

"Wa'er. Nee' a glath wa'er."

"There's a spigot on the side of the house. You're not to go inside."

I stumbled toward it. A water hole in the

46

desert. Or a mirage. Until I touched the rusty handle, I was sure it would disappear. The water wasn't cold and it tasted like metal, but I drank it out of my hands until I thought my belly would burst.

I staggered back down the hill, burping. Even with the funnel, I spilled some gas on the lawn. It took four hard yanks, but the green machine roared back to life.

Cut on, and on. And on. Back and forth, side to side, watch for stones, keep a neat row.

I wanted to stop. Just leave the machine and go home. Nobody at home knew I had a job so nobody would know I quit. This is torture. Who needs it? I'm walking on burning needles. My blisters have blisters. Hammers banging on my shoulders. Electric jolts in my wrists. I can feel every inch of me, and every inch of me hurts. Just stop and walk away.

A long black car swept down the driveway, stopped and honked. Dr. Kahn stuck his head out the window, yelled something at me, then drove down to the county road and out of sight.

I could leave now.

You've got to do it, Captain Marks. You're the

only one who can make it through the renegades to Fort Desolation and bring back the Regiment. We're counting on you.

And then suddenly I didn't hurt anymore, and I couldn't have stopped if I wanted to. All I could do was go back and forth, back and forth, and sometimes I ran into the bushes along the side of the lawn, the sharp thorns snagging on my sleeves and whipping at my chest and scratching the back of my hands until blood bubbled up in the thin red lines, and twice I stepped into holes and fell down and stones clattered against the whirling blade and bounced off my legs, and when the mower ran out of gas again I filled it and yanked it back to life and pushed on, and on, and I stumbled along like I was drunk.

"You call this mowing a lawn?"

I was halfway between the porch and the county road. I had cut half the front lawn, what was he talking about? I followed his long, quivering finger up the hill. The lawn was a mess. I had missed hundreds of tufts of grass. Most of the rows were squiggly light green snakes lying among darker green patches of uncut grass. The work of a crazy drunken lawn mower.

"I call this a disgrace."

He lifted the mower and examined the blade. "You must have gone out of your way to find every stone on the lawn. Look at the chips on the blade. I'll have to get another one. Cost at least four fifty." He shook his head. "That'll be subtracted from your wages, of course."

He looked at his watch. "Well, it's after three o'clock. Tomorrow you'll do it all over again. What did you say?"

I hadn't said a word. I turned away so he couldn't see me cry, and I stumbled down to the county road.

5

I don't remember walking around the lake. Car horns kept warning me off the road back to the sandy shoulder. The road shimmered and heaved in the heat. Twice I stopped to throw up, but nothing came out. I saw the sign, Marino's Beach Club and Snack Bar, and staggered right up to the serving counter.

"Wa'er? Pleath?"

Connie said, "You got to be kidding. You want water, go jump in the lake."

"Hey, wait a minute." A big bronze chest with a St. Christopher medal hanging between huge muscles loomed up. "You Michelle's brother?"

"Yek."

"Connie, get him some water." Big hard arms

grabbed me around the chest and dragged me to a picnic table under the shade of a beach umbrella. "Your sister's been looking for you, she drove past here twice. Connie!"

"I only got two hands, Peter."

"Since when? C'mon, this boy needs water."

"M'okay," I said.

"You'll be all right, just a little heatstroke. You've been running or something? Heavy fella like you shouldn't run in this weather." He held a cup to my mouth while I drank. "What happened to your hands? Cat scratch you up?"

"Yeah."

"Come with me." He helped me around the back of the snack bar shack to a small room. "Here you go." He lowered me on a cot and opened a first-aid cabinet.

Connie came in with more water and some big white pills. "Salt tablets," she said. "Make you feel better."

"Thanks."

Pete poured alcohol on the back of my hands.

"It stings."

"A man can take it. So you're the famous kid

brother. Just lie down now. That's it. You know who I am?''

"Pete Marino.''

"The one and only.'' He grinned. "So. What really happened to you? The Rummies work you over?''

"No . . . I . . . I was running. I fell down.''

"Hey, you can tell Peter the Great. Look, it happens to every summer kid at least once. Even happened to me.''

"What happened?''

"About four, five years ago. I was your age. They caught me alone on the other side of the lake and gave me a pounding. Must have been eight of them, the whole Rumson gang. I went back with my brother Vinnie and a couple of his friends and we cleaned 'em out. They haven't bothered a Marino since.''

"Why do they beat up summer kids?''

"Who knows? They're crazy.'' He whirled his finger near his head. "The whole lake, all this land around here, used to belong to the Rumson family, but they're so dumb they lost it. Hey, listen, I better get you home.''

"I can make it.''

52

"It's a long walk."

"You know where I live?"

"Are you kidding? C'mon." He helped me up and led me outside. He was holding me up more than he had to. People playing in the water and lying on the beach turned to look at me. I felt foolish. "Connie! I'll be right back, I'm going to drive Bobby Marks home."

"We got people waiting to rent boats."

"You got two hands. You told me so yourself." He opened the door of a white pickup truck. I had seen it before, it was famous around the lake. The doors and roof and bed of the truck were covered with red lightning bolts on which was lettered, in blue script, THE MARINO EXPRESS. He had to boost me up into the cab I was so tired and sore.

He jerked the truck out of the gravel parking lot onto the county road, but once he was on the road he drove slowly, like he was leading a ticker-tape parade. All along the lake, girls and boys, kids and old people, waved and yelled his name. A lot of people noticed me in the truck. I felt good about that.

He turned up our hill, and I said, "You can let

me off anywhere," but he just grinned and said, "Door-to-door service." Michelle was just getting out of our Dodge when we pulled into the driveway. Pete jumped out almost before he stopped.

"Marks residence?"

"Pete! What are you doing here?" Michelle looked happy and scared at the same time.

"Special delivery." Pete danced around the truck. He was barefoot. He opened the door and hauled me out, and even though I could walk he made a big show of half-carrying me to the lawn. "Think you can make it the rest of the way, big fella?"

"Where'd you find him?" asked Michelle.

My mother came out of the house then, her eyes wide, and she started toward me with her arms out. I didn't want a big scene in front of Pete, so I used my last ounce of energy to run past her and go inside. Through the window, I saw Mom glance at Michelle and Pete, who were standing very close talking. Then she came inside.

"Are you all right?"

"M'okay." I felt like all the blood and water

had run out of my body. My bones had turned to rubber. I was hot and cold at the same time.

"What happened?"

"Nothing."

"Nothing? Where were you?"

"Around the lake. I was running and I fell down."

"You were running? From whom?"

"Just running. I'm going to take a nap."

"Do you want something to eat or drink?"

"No."

"Oh, Bobby, you must be sick." She followed me into my bedroom. I fell on my bed. She was taking off my sneakers when I fainted. The last thing I thought of before I passed out was lunch. I hadn't eaten my lunch.

It was the first time in my life I ever missed a meal.

6

Robert Marks was melting.

Wetly, he stirred in his bed. He held his breath and listened to the darkness.

Drip.

He was melting away.

Drip.

Fourteen years of butterfat, heavy cream, noodle casseroles, butterscotch, fudge, congealed grease, peanut butter, side orders, lamb chops, double blubber, pound cake with ice cream, excess baggage, Popsicles, mint patties, were leaking down the drain. Robert Marks was melting down to his true self. Sword-lean and rawhide-tough.

Drip.

They would find him in the morning, thin and

sinewy, a St. Christopher medal on his muscular chest. Underneath all that fat he had always been as hard as a rock. His family would wail for Robert Marks—well, his mother would wail for sure—and the police would shake their heads. It wasn't a murder, it was only a subtraction. Newspaper reporters would elbow into the bedroom, dragging their feet through the sizzling puddles of fat that Robert Marks had once worn in disguise.

The nosy reporters would poke at his books, pull out his records, open his games, lift up the stamps in his album to make sure he'd pasted them onto the right spaces. They would find his secret drawer and read all the stories he had started. They would go through his desk looking for photographs of the late, large, unlamented Robert Marks. They would check his radio to see which station he had been listening to. They would study the maps on his walls and the notes on his bulletin board.

He would sit on the edge of the bed watching them, posing his new razor-sharp jaw, only one chin, for the cameras.

"Okay, slim," one of them would snarl, "where'd you stash the fat boy?"

"I'm just a shadow of what he was," he would coolly reply.

"That's not good enough, slats," snarled another, "I want all the news that's fit to print."

His father would push in. "Robert Marks would never fit in print, or anywhere else."

His mother would push in. "Leave the poor boy alone. Whoever he is, he hasn't had breakfast yet."

Dr. Kahn would push in. "What makes you think this isn't the same summer boy who can't even mow a lawn?"

My pillowcase and sheets were sopping wet. Michelle was sitting in a chair alongside the bed, her head on her chest. She was asleep. A book, *Catcher in the Rye*, was open on her lap. The clock read 2:15. It was dark outside.

I tried to get up, but my legs were too heavy to move. Polio. I tried with all my might, and fell back asleep.

"You look much better." My mother put her lips to my forehead. "And your head's cool."

"I feel fine."

"I have to go to the library this morning. You just rest. Michelle's here. And the refrigerator's full."

"Okay."

She stopped at the door. "Your father called last night. He insists you go back to day camp."

"I won't go."

"Well, we'll think of something when I get back." She smiled and blew me a kiss.

I waited until I heard the car leave before I tried to get out of bed. My legs worked. But I almost screamed when my feet touched the floor. Blisters. On my heels and big toes. There were blisters on my hands. Every muscle ached. Just breathing hurt my ribs. What a mess. I feel like the lawn looks.

I hobbled into the kitchen. Congratulations, Captain, you made it. I opened the refrigerator and relaxed in the sweet chill. I gulped orange juice from the bottle. I tore off pieces from last night's chicken and stuffed them in my mouth. I bit into a tomato and I scooped out some cottage cheese with my fingers and worked it into the last free space between my teeth and my cheek.

While I was chewing I grabbed a piece of seeded rye bread and folded it over a lump of Swiss cheese and pickle chips. I began to feel human again.

"Bobby? I'm leaving now." Michelle came into the kitchen. "Did Pete say anything about me?"

"Uh uh." I closed the refrigerator door so she could see I couldn't talk because my mouth was full.

"Ugh," she said as a piece of pickle chip slipped out of my mouth. "Well, at least you're back to normal."

7

I didn't get to Dr. Kahn's until nearly eleven o'clock that morning, but this time I was prepared. I wore heavy shoes with high socks to help protect my legs against flying stones. My father's work gloves. A baseball cap. Sunglasses. I had two bologna sandwiches, cookies, a Milky Way candy bar and two oranges in a brown paper bag. It took me fifteen minutes to climb up the driveway because I tried to walk on the sides of my feet so I wouldn't step on the blisters.

Dr. Kahn was standing on the porch talking to Willie Rumson. A cigarette dangled from the corner of Willie's mouth. He looked at me over his shoulder. "Here comes The Thing."

Dr. Kahn said, "I didn't think you were coming back."

"I'm sorry I'm late," I said.

"Too late," said Willie. "*Semper fi*, fats, the Marines have landed." When he talked, his cigarette stuck to his lower lip.

"I haven't made a decision yet," said Dr. Kahn. "First of all, Willie, you were not reliable last summer. I don't like a boy who is not reliable."

"Look at this lawn," said Willie. "Makes me want to puke."

"Second of all, a dollar twenty-five is too high."

"I thought I told you to take a hike, fats."

"Are you trying to intimidate this boy?" Dr. Kahn's voice rose. "On my property?"

"Take it easy, Doc. You want your lawn lookin' good? Or like we fought a war on it?"

"I'll give you a dollar an hour."

"A dollar an hour? To a vet?"

"Veteran of a reform school, more likely," said Dr. Kahn.

Willie straightened up. His ropy arms were so

long they reached his knees. "Wake up, Doc. You know how much they're paying at the laundry? To start?"

"Whatever it is, I suggest you take it."

"Well, you know what you can do with your lawn." He hooked his thumbs around a web belt with a shiny brass buckle. "You're making a bad mistake, Doc, a *bad* mistake."

"Are you threatening me?" Dr. Kahn was almost shouting. "Get off my property or I'll call the police."

"You do that, Doc." Willie swaggered down the porch steps. "Ask for my Uncle Homer, he's the sergeant."

"Off my property!"

"Don't bust a gut." Willie laughed out of the corner of his mouth. He shoved me with his shoulder as he passed me. He lowered his voice. "And you, pig meat, you're making a *really* bad mistake. You ever see me coming, you better pray. Give your soul to God, fats, 'cause your ass belongs to me."

"What did you say to that boy?"

Over his shoulder, Willie said, "I wished him

good luck, Doc. He's gonna need it working for you.''

We watched Willie walk toward his car. He rocked from side to side, head and shoulders hunched forward like a cowboy walking to a showdown. He gunned his Chevy down the driveway, firing gravel, and spun onto the county road on two wheels. We could hear him screeching around the lake.

"Don't concern yourself with him, boy. I'm the one you have to deal with." Dr. Kahn motioned me up to the porch. "I'm going to be watching you. Like a hawk. There are plenty of others who would give their eyeteeth for this job. But I believe in giving a boy a second chance.''

"I'll do my best.''

"You'll do better than that. Now get the mower. Don't forget to check the gas and oil. Watch for stones. I had a new blade put on, which you paid for.'' He turned and walked into the house. But I felt his eyes for the rest of the day.

It wasn't as bad as the first day, but it was bad enough. Each of the blisters on my feet broke, pop, one at a time, then stung for a while as the water was absorbed by my socks. I walked on raw skin. I tried not to hold the grips too hard, but the blisters on my hands broke, too, and I grew new ones wherever there was any skin left. The gloves helped a little. At least I couldn't see what my hands looked like. Hamburger, probably. Handsburger?

First, I went over all the patches I missed yesterday, then I started cutting in rows again, back and forth, side to side. I really concentrated. I watched for stones, and when I saw one I stopped, picked it up, and piled it on the edge of the driveway. If I found a stone in the middle of the row, I carried it to the end in my pocket. Even the little stones were a tight fit, and pinched my legs and backside. I watched for holes, too. I was very careful.

The longer I cut, the bigger the lawn seemed to get. A friend of my father's once showed us his color movies of a mule trip down into the Grand Canyon. He said that the farther down he went, the bigger the canyon seemed to get. From the top, it looked like just a huge hole, but as he descended, the walls of the canyon seemed to flatten back and the hole became another world. It was something like that with the lawn. After a couple of hours, I could see that I had come a long way, but the distance between me and the county road didn't seem to shrink that much. At the twelve-o'clock fire siren, I shut off the motor and went up to the porch to eat lunch.

"You're the slowest lawn boy I've ever had," said Dr. Kahn. "At this rate it'll take you most of the week just to cut the grass."

I shrugged because I felt bad and didn't know what to say.

"Obviously, you don't care. Do you want this job?"

"Yes."

"Then prove it to me."

I didn't finish my lunch, but I wasn't too hungry. The first bologna sandwich stuck in my mouth, and I forced it down with juice I sucked out of my orange. I ate the candy bar for quick energy, and hit the lawn.

I tried to go faster, but then I went over a stone. Clang. The blade batted it against a tree. Thud. I got panicky. The rest of the afternoon was a blur. The heat was pounding me into the ground, and my clothes stuck to me. My underwear was strangling me. Sweat pouring down my forehead stung my eyes and blinded me. My hands and feet were burning. My lungs were bursting. I tried to think of Captain Marks, but now the whole daydream seemed dumb. I'm the slowest officer in the U.S. Cavalry. By the time I get to the fort, the stagecoach will be a burned-out wreck, the Colonel's daughter kidnapped and my whole troop will be spread-eagled on the sand waiting for the red ants.

I thought three o'clock would never come. I cut two more rows just in case my watch was running on its usual low Basal time, and then I pulled the mower up to the shed. Dr. Kahn was waiting for me.

"What am I going to do about you?"

"I don't know."

"Are you sure you want this job?"

"Yes."

"How can I pay you seventy-five cents an hour when you're not doing seventy-five cents an hour's worth of work?"

I shook my head.

"You seem like a decent boy," said Dr. Kahn. "I want to give you every opportunity to prove yourself. But obviously I can't pay you top dollar. I might allow you to keep working, on a strict trial, of course, for fifty cents an hour. Well?"

"Okay."

"Tomorrow. Nine A.M. Sharp."

For the second day in a row, I turned away before he could see me cry.

8

Our house wasn't directly on Rumson Lake, but from the old swing in the backyard I could see the island gathering shadows in the late afternoon sunlight, a darkening clump of trees in the middle of a ring of sparkling water.

When I swung up high enough I caught glimpses of swimmers splashing out from shore. They were so cool and I was so hot. I was jealous of people who didn't have to think about how their bodies looked without clothes. When I was younger I was a good swimmer. My father and Michelle taught me. But after I started feeling embarrassed about my body, I made excuses not to go swimming. When I did go, I tried to stay underwater as long as possible so people couldn't see me. Last summer there was an underwater swimming contest at Marino's Beach, and I'm sure I would have won, but you had to start from the low board. I wasn't afraid of jumping off the low board, but I didn't want to walk out on it while people were looking me over.

I pumped hard on the swing and made my own breeze. That cooled me off. I used to spend a lot of time on this swing. When you really get going on a swing, the rest of the world fades away and you can imagine yourself anybody anywhere. I once had a daydream in which I was the invisible boy. Whenever I wanted to be invisible I just drank a special potion I had concocted in a chemistry lab. At first, I mostly used my invisibility to solve crimes by eavesdropping on criminals while they were making their plans. There are problems in being invisible. You have to be very careful crossing streets since drivers can't see you. You can eat only when nobody's around. If a sandwich suddenly jumps off a plate and disappears, you could give yourself away. Especially if you're on a criminal case. Crooks aren't all that dumb, you know. Once they suspect there's an invisible person spying on them, they'll lock the doors, shut off the lights so you can't see them either, and keep feeling around the room until they catch you.

About a year ago, in that daydream, I started using my invisibility to sneak into the girls' locker room at school. In the beginning I just sort of skulked around the locker room, watching them undress, but then I got bolder and stood very close, and every so often I might touch someone. In my daydreams, they never screamed or ran away. I would get good warm feelings that started in my belly and flowed down. Sometimes, if I was alone in the house, or in a locked bathroom, I would stroke myself until the warm feelings became a throbbing drumbeat that exploded.

I told Joanie about the invisible boy, which was a mistake. She has a very logical mind, and she asked me one question which spoiled everything: Does drinking the chemical make your clothes invisible, too, or do you have to walk around naked to be invisible? I told her the chemical affected everything you touch, so your clothes would be invisible, too. But later, thinking it over, I realized it made no sense. What if you touched another person? Would she start to disappear, too?

So you'd have to be naked. And what would

happen if you misjudged the amount of chemical you drank, if you didn't drink enough to last until you got back to the lab? Or if you were delayed getting back to the lab by heavy traffic? You might suddenly become visible again, maybe in the middle of the street, maybe even in the girls' locker room. And you'd be stark naked. And everybody would see you.

I never had that daydream again.

Joanie. I wondered what she was doing in the city. It wasn't like her to be so mysterious, or so nervous. I wondered if somebody was sick and had to go to the doctor, something so terrible she couldn't even talk about it. It might have been just a family secret. Her parents are funny sometimes. But we always told each other family secrets.

Yet, I was also kind of glad she wasn't around. I can imagine how she would have reacted to the way Dr. Kahn treated me. She would have gotten very angry for me. He's taking advantage of you, Bob, he has no right to do that, you can't let him do that, you have to stand up for your rights or people will just walk all over you. Are you a man or a rug?

I would flop down on the floor and open my mouth. I'm a bearskin rug, I'd say.

It's no joke, she'd snap. It was bad enough you let him cheat you out of twenty-five cents an hour, the sign on the bulletin board said one dollar. But once you both agreed on seventy-five cents, well, a deal is a deal.

It was fifty cents or nothing, I'd say. Fifty cents is better than nothing.

It you stood up to him like a man you'd get your seventy-five cents, she would say. If he really didn't like your work he would have fired you. Obviously, he can't get anybody else at even a dollar an hour.

You just don't understand, I'd say.

I understand one thing, she'd say. If he thinks you're just a rug, he'll walk all over you. Next time it'll be twenty-five cents an hour. Now, tomorrow, you tell him...

That's Joanie. Once in class I got caught with a note one of the hoods told me to pass to his girlfriend. The teacher snatched it away from me, tore it up and told me to stay after school. Joanie made me go up after class and explain what had happened. I didn't have to stay after school, but the hood beat me up on the way home. Joanie said she was sorry I got beat up, but it was more important to show that no one could take advantage of me. I really showed them, didn't I?

Swinging, I got a little mad at her. She got me into this whole mess in the first place. If she had kept to our deal, I could be spending the summer working on a nice little project for school, no Dr. Kahn and no Willie Rumson.

I went into the house and had a meat loaf sandwich with mayonnaise. And a glass of orange soda. I was still eating when my mother came home, carrying books.

"Bobby! We're going to eat in a little while. You'll spoil your dinner."

"No, I won't. You'll see."

"How was your day?"

"Just fine."

"What did you do?"

"Oh, I worked on the project. With Joanie."

"Oh?" She put her books down on the kitchen table and poured herself a glass of orange soda. She poured a little more soda into my glass and sat down. "Bobby?"

"Yeah?"

"Sit down." She looked very serious. "The one thing I won't stand for is being lied to."

Dumb. I really stepped into that one. Of course she must know that Joanie and her parents went back to the city.

Michelle burst into the kitchen. "What a day. Those little brats are . . ." She stopped when she saw us sitting together. "Is this a secret meeting or can I join in?"

"You might as well sit down, too. What did you do today, Bobby? The Millers are in the city."

"Well, I was going to surprise you. I've got a job."

"What kind of job?"

Michelle's Barnard sweatshirt gave me the idea. "I'm helping out Pete Marino."

Michelle's eyes got wide, but she didn't say anything.

"Doing what?"

"Oh, just sort of helping around. Sweeping up. He's not going to pay me right away, but after I learn how to make sandwiches and collect money for the boats, he'll pay me top dollar. Now I'm just sort of in training."

"Is that going to last all summer?"

"If I want it. When Joanie comes back I'll decide if I want to stay or work on the project with her. So I wasn't really lying. I've been working on the project in my mind."

"I'm not sure your father will be satisfied with that."

"It's too late to get into camp anyway."

"I'm sure we can still get you in."

I jumped up. "I feel like cutting the grass."

"You do?" My mother looked surprised.

"Sure. *Duz* does everything. I want to surprise Dad."

"You sure will," said Michelle.

"Why should he have to cut the grass after a tough week in the city?" While they were looking at each other I ran out and got the mower.

A narrow escape. I probably should have told Mom the truth. She would have helped me convince Dad. But then she would have interfered, driven over to look at Dr. Kahn's lawn, maybe even talked to Dr. Kahn. I wanted this to be all mine.

I cut grass like a demon and finished in a half hour, a world's record for me. We didn't have much lawn. Nothing to it for a professional.

Michelle talked through dinner about the kids in her group at camp. She had the four year olds, boys and girls, and half of them sat and whined, and the other half kept running into the bushes. Mom didn't seem too interested, but I kept asking questions so Michelle would keep talking. The conversation never got back to me and my job.

That night, Michelle came into my room and closed the door.

"Okay, what's the story? You're not working at the snack bar."

"Says who?"

"I'd know, believe me. What are you doing?"

"Do you swear you won't tell?"

"No."

"Then forget it."

"Look, Bobby, if you're doing something bad, or dangerous, I can't keep it a secret. I won't take that responsibility."

She looked as if she really cared. I told her about Dr. Kahn's lawn, but I left out a lot of the painful details.

"How much is he paying you?"

"Fifty cents an hour."

"That's all?"

"It's better than nothing."

"I guess so." She turned to study my wall. "Does Pete Marino know all this?"

"No."

"Pete Marino's a very honest person. Pete Marino's not going to lie for you."

Just the way she repeated his name, like she loved to say it, gave me the idea.

"I figured you'd talk to him for me."

"Me?"

"That's right. If you do that for me, then . . . well, you might want me to help you out someday, and I would."

She just turned and stared at me, the way they do in the movies just before they say "That's blackmail." She didn't say that, she just nodded. "I'll see what I can do."

"A deal's a deal," I said.

9

Nine A.M. Sharp. High Basal Time. My watch read 8:55. I rolled the green machine out of the shed, started it on the third try, and attacked the lawn. Good-bye, grass, here comes the quickest blade on Rumson Lake.

Cutting grass isn't boring if you have the right attitude. Now, if you keep looking at your watch, or thinking about all the things you'd rather be doing than pushing a heavy mower back and forth, back and forth, you'll probably go out of your mind. But if you can understand that the grass is your enemy, that every row you cut brings you that much closer to victory, you might still go crazy but the time will pass much faster. One moment a huge lawn will be sneering greenly at you, a moment later you'll notice that more than half the lawn is a lighter green than it was when you started. You're more than halfway finished. And that last row, the very last time you stagger from one side of the lawn to the other, is like a victory lap after winning a race. It's so sweet you forget that your back is broken, your legs are lead, your arms are dead and your hands are locked forever into curled claws that fit only the handles of a lawn mower.

At exactly 2:17 P.M., HBT, Wednesday, July 9, 1952, I beat Dr. Kahn's lawn. I left that chlorophyll monster chopped to size, one and a half inches high.

I took a minute to savor my triumph, imagine the brass bands and the cheering crowds. Ladies and gentlemen, the new heavyweight champion of mowing, Big Bob Marks.

One minute was all I got. At 2:18 P.M., Dr. Kahn without a word handed me a pair of giant hedge clippers and pointed to the bushes that bordered the lawn.

Snip, snip, snip, snip. Muscles I had never annoyed before, in my chest, upper arms and forearms, began to complain. A new crop of blisters tried to grow on my palms, but most of them didn't make it through the old blisters. Sorry, fellas, it's first come first serve on these tough old hands.

At 3:05 P.M., HBT, when I returned the mower and the clippers to the shed, Dr. Kahn didn't say a word to me. Not a single word from the evil Dr. K. I left him speechless. That's praise from the devil, Big Bob.

I dragged myself around the lake and collapsed on a stool at the snack bar. If ever a boy deserved a frosted malted, it was me, right now. But the thought of anything to eat gave me a stomach-ache. Most of my lunch was still in the bag on Dr. Kahn's porch. Connie glared at me until I ordered a lemonade. I finished it in three gulps, then pretended I was still drinking until Pete saw me and came over. He had some scratches on his shoulder, and a purple bruise on his neck. I wondered if he got them making out with Michelle.

Pete whispered, "Michelle told me."

She must have sneaked out of the house last night after Mom and I went to bed.

"Is it okay?" I asked.

"Bob, I hate to lie," he said. "My father

would be mad as hell. Connie and I are supposed to be running a business here."

"It's just for a couple of days. Until the weekend. When my father comes up I'll tell him the truth."

"Why do you have to lie in the first place?"

"He doesn't have any confidence in me." I was surprised at how easy it was to talk to Pete. "He's always afraid I'll get hurt, or do a bad job and embarrass him."

"And you want to show him."

"Once he sees I can do the job, it'll be all right, he'll let me."

Pete clapped a hand on my shoulder. "That's the spirit, big fella. You're going to show your Dad he can be proud of you."

Now that would really be a record, I thought. But I just said, "That's right."

"What if your mother calls you here?"

"You could tell her I took a walk or something. Or that I'm in swimming."

He shook his head. "I really want to help, I really do. But I hate to lie."

"Well." I tried to look as if I hated to lie, too.

"Michelle and I made this deal to help each other out."

He squinted at me. "How are you going to help her?"

"Well, like I'd do the same thing for her someday." I got very busy fishing in my pocket for money so I wouldn't have to look him in the eye. "Like if she had any secrets or something, I wouldn't tell anybody."

"Yeah. Right." He didn't look too happy about that, and I wondered now if he didn't like me anymore. I almost wished he'd say "No deal," or maybe "Let's do this right, Bob, why don't you come work here for real?" But he said, "Okay. But just till the weekend."

"Thanks a lot."

He grinned. "You betchum, Red Ryder. Connie! Lemonade's on the house for my pard here." He rapped my arm in a real friendly way, winked, and went off to take care of a rowboat customer. Connie waited until he was gone before she asked me for my dime.

Michelle seemed nervous at dinner, and Mom's mind was somewhere else, so there wasn't much conversation. It was Michelle's night to do the dishes. I went into my room and turned on the radio. Nothing but baseball games on every station. The Yankees, the Dodgers and the Giants. It was such a clear night, I even got games in Philadelphia and Boston. I really didn't enjoy listening to baseball games, but I never told too many people besides Joanie, who thought they were a big bore, too. Especially if you're a lousy player like me and have to pretend you're a big fan or the other guys call you a fag. All real men are supposed to love baseball. For a while I thought there was something wrong with me, not even liking baseball, but then I figured it this way: If all you have to do to prove you're a regular guy is pretend you like baseball, memorize some batting averages and argue if Joe DiMaggio is better than Ted Williams then it isn't a real test. I saw a war movie once where a German spy got away with his disguise for a long time because he knew the score of every World Series game ever played. All the real American soldiers thought he was a great guy. They finally caught him because he didn't know Legs Diamond was a gangster. He thought it was the nickname of a movie actress. Well, at least he wasn't a fag, just a phoney.

When I was about eleven my father took me to a Giants game. I don't even remember who they were playing, but I remember he got mad because I kept asking for hot dogs and ice cream whenever the game got interesting. I don't think he was all that involved in the game, either, but the people sitting around us kept making remarks about how much I was eating, and that annoyed my father. Not at them for making the remarks, but at me for giving people something to criticize.

My father's very particular. He likes things just right. He can't stand it if the pillows on the sofa are messed up, or the car is dusty or his newspaper is wrinkled before he gets a chance to read it. Since my mother started studying to be a teacher he's really been complaining about how she sometimes leaves books out, open, with a pencil between the pages she's reading. Michelle thinks he doesn't like the idea of her getting a job, but I think he just doesn't like an untidy pile.

The teakettle started whistling. I heard Mom go into the kitchen, pour her tea, and walk back to her bedroom. She'd be asleep pretty soon. I kept spinning the dial, but I couldn't find a station with the kind of songs I liked. "Tennessee Waltz" and "Come On-a My House" and "Mockin' Bird Hill" and "My Truly, Truly Fair." Or Eddie Fisher singing anything, he was my favorite.

So I just lay in bed and listened to my body for a while. If you concentrate, while you're feeling your body, you can hear it, too. Your stomach doesn't just hurt, it gurgles like water going through pipes. While your muscles are aching because they've been stretched, you can hear them squeak back into regular shape. Heart thumps, of course, bone crackles, and if you're lucky, you can sometimes hear your brain waves bang against the inside of your skull. That would be like tuning in Chicago; you can't be sure you'll get it. I heard a lot of noise from the old body; I was so tired and every part of me was complaining. But it was a good kind of hurt because I knew I had really done a job on that lawn today.

After a while, I started to drift off. A car came up the hill, moving fast in high gear, then slowed to shift into a lower gear to get to the top.

Usually, at the top, cars speed up again, but this one stopped. I heard the screen door close softly. Michelle was sneaking out of the house. Was that Pete outside in the Marino Express? I thought I'd try to stay awake to check out what time she came back, but I never made it. I think I fell asleep while the car was turning around to go back down the hill.

On Thursday, Dr. Kahn had me down on my hands and knees most of the morning pulling out tiny blades of grass growing up through the gravel driveway. I started out wearing gloves, but the thick fingers were too clumsy to grab the little shoots. I used my thumb and forefinger like tweezers, pick, pick, pick, the way Michelle plucks her eyebrows. The gravel kept digging into my kneecaps until both of them were scraped. My back was breaking. For a while I made believe I was prospecting for gold, but that got boring pretty soon. If gold was that hard to get, who needs it?

I ate only half my sandwich for lunch. The greasy salami made me nauseous in the heat. In the afternoon I washed Dr. Kahn's long black

Buick, and that should have been fun except he kept peering over my shoulder.

"Wipe, don't rub," he said. "You rub like that, one grain of sand, just one grain in that cloth, you'll scratch the finish. You want to pay for a new paint job?"

I shook my head.

"Then keep the cloth slightly damp, and wipe, one continuous motion." He made one continuous motion with his arm. He looked like a one-winged hawk about to take off. Didn't he have anything better to do than watch me?

I did the dishes Thursday night, and Michelle left right after dinner. She said she was going to visit her girlfriend across the lake, and then go with her to a counselors' meeting. Another counselors' meeting? I'll bet. Probably go to the island. This time I didn't even bother turning on the radio. I think I fell asleep before my head hit the pillow.

On Friday morning there was a truck parked at the top of Dr. Kahn's driveway, a rusty green pickup with sloppy red lettering on the driver's door. JACK SMITH AND SONS LANDSCAPING. RUMSON LAKE-9-9448. The open bed of the truck was filled with rakes, hoes, bushel baskets, shovels, chicken wire and bales of fertilizer. Three men I had never seen before were crawling around the flower beds. One was a short, stumpy old man in overalls and a plaid shirt. He was puffing on a pipe and grunting as he smoothed earth around a cluster of yellow flowers. So that was the famous Jack Smith who decked his foreman. I guess you don't have to look like a hero to be one. Of course, he was a lot younger when he saved the baby.

The other two looked like his sons. They were both around twenty, tall and lean, and they weren't wearing shirts, even though it wasn't too warm yet. They had smooth, tanned skins pulled tight over muscles that flexed and popped as they weeded. And lots of veins.

For a minute I felt scared and angry. Dr. Kahn called them to replace me, I thought, I'm going to be fired, but then I remembered he had said he had a weekly gardening service.

As I passed them, they all looked up. Old Jack Smith just moved his teeth so that his pipe nodded at me. One of his sons said, "You still here, beach ball?"

The other one said, "But you better be rollin' along," and they both laughed.

"Boy, come over here," called Dr. Kahn. He pointed toward the swimming pool. "There's brushes and soap and a mop in the cabana closet. I want that deck shining."

I was glad to be off by myself. It was nice and quiet up at the pool. There was a little white house, just big enough to change clothes in, with a bathroom and a closet filled with cleaning equipment. There were three white iron tables with closed umbrellas in the middle, and a dozen wrought-iron chairs arranged on a white tile deck that surrounded the pool, which wasn't too big. Pete Marino could cross it in two strokes. I could probably go back and forth underwater twice without coming up for air. Maybe three times. Except for a few leaves floating on the surface, the water was clear.

I scrubbed the tiles with soapy water, careful not to let any of it slop into the pool, then mopped until the wet tiles glistened in the sun. It looked nice.

"Huh," said Dr. Kahn. I hadn't heard him come up behind me.

"Is this okay?"

He nodded and walked away. It must really look nice. I felt good about that. I washed out the brush and the mop and the pail, and put them back into the closet. When I came out of the cabana, there were black footprints all over my clean deck. I heard the Smith boys laughing.

I did it all over again, and this time I didn't put the stuff away, I just stood guard at the pool until Dr. Kahn came back.

"Are you going to look at this all day?" he asked.

"What should I do next?"

"I don't like a boy who doesn't have initiative. There are a thousand things to do to make this place look beautiful for the weekend. Sweep the porch, wash the garbage pails, get the leaves out of the gutters. Just look around, you'll find things."

The porch was easy, and so were the garbage pails, but the gutters scared me. I hate to climb ladders, and the gutters, long wooden troughs that catch the rainwater running off the roof, were pretty high. I found a ladder in the shed, a long wooden one with round rungs, and set it against the house. I started feeling shaky on the

91

third rung, but as long as I didn't look down I was all right. The gutters weren't really clogged, just a few leaves and acorns and junk the rain had washed off the roof. I had forgotten to bring a bag up, so I stuffed it all in my pockets. There seemed to be more room than usual in my pockets.

"What's this ladder doing here, Jim?" It was one of the Smith boys.

"Let's put it away," said Jim. He started to shake the ladder.

"Hey, I'm up here," I shouted.

"You hear that, Jim?"

"Hear what?"

"That sound."

"Let go of the ladder," I yelled.

"There it is again." They were really shaking the ladder now.

"Cut it out." I nearly lost my balance and grabbed the gutters.

"Okay, Jim, one, two, three, heave."

The ladder was moving out from under me. I grabbed for the roof. My knees hit the gutter. There was a cracking sound as the gutter broke loose from the edge of the roof. But I scrambled up on the roof just in time. The ladder toppled slowly over, crushing a few flowers.

"Let's just leave it there, Jim. I feel like walking around that nice clean pool again."

It was pleasant up on the roof. A good view of Rumson Lake sparkling in the afternoon sun and the low green foothills beyond. I could see meadows and farmhouses and the tiny brown and black dots that were grazing cows and horses. Dr. Kahn's place looked beautiful from the roof. My lawn was velvety green, the hedges thick and neat. After a while I heard the clatter of tools being tossed into the back of the pickup, then I saw the green truck roll down the driveway. I thought a long tan arm sticking out of the passenger window waved to me.

If I didn't have to worry about getting down, I really wouldn't have minded being up on the roof. The sun felt good, and the roof wasn't so steep I had to worry about rolling off. I lay on my back and watched a chicken hawk glide and roll in the sky. That's freedom, flying.

"Are you sleeping on the job?"

"The ladder fell down, Dr. Kahn."

"Right on the geraniums." He set the ladder

against the house. "Come on, come on, slow-poke, time's money."

Less than a penny a minute, you old miser. I can afford to spend an extra thirty seconds coming down the ladder so I don't fall and crack my skull.

"How did you manage this little trick?" I'd forgotten how black and deep his eyes could get.

"The ladder fell."

He shook his head. "I will not reward clumsiness. You will be docked for the time you were sunbathing on the roof. How long were you up there? A half hour?"

"Dr. Kahn, it wasn't my fault." That came out before I had a chance to stop it.

"I don't like a boy who makes excuses."

"It's the truth. Those Smith boys knocked over the ladder. While I was on it. I had to jump on the roof."

"Why would they do that?"

"I don't know." I couldn't tell him that I thought it was because they were friends of Willie Rumson, the boy he didn't hire. "I guess it was their idea of a practical joke."

"That's not my idea of humor at all, damage a

gutter, ruin flowers, waste time. This time I won't hold you responsible.'' He walked away.

I finished the gutters and put away the ladder and mopped the new black footprints on the tile pool deck. By that time it was a few minutes after three o'clock. I knocked on the front door.

''Well?''

''I'm all done.''

He stared at me. ''I suppose you want to be paid.''

''Yes, sir.''

He disappeared back inside. I waited about a nickel's worth before he came back with a handful of crumpled dollar bills and a small leather change purse. He counted out seven dollars and eighty-seven cents.

''For the whole week?''

''On Monday you worked six hours at seventy-five cents an hour, which is four dollars and fifty cents, minus thirty-eight cents for your half hour lunch break and four dollars and fifty cents for the broken mower blade. On Monday afternoon you owed me thirty-eight cents.

''On Tuesday you received no pay since you had to redo Monday's work. On Wednesday,

Thursday and Friday, at fifty cents an hour, you earned three dollars per day, minus twenty-five cents for each day for lunch.''

He droned on. I barely heard him. Seven dollars and eighty-seven cents for the whole week. ''If you want me to add it all up for you . . .''

''That's okay.''

''I'm sure you will find it quite correct. I am a doctor of mathematics and until my retirement I supervised the actuarial tables of one of the largest insurance firms. Do you know what I'm talking about?''

''I thought you were a real doctor.''

''I've decided not to dock you for your time on the roof, or for the damage to the gutter and the flowers. I believe your story about the Smiths. However,'' he raised a bony finger, ''I must warn you that I do not like a boy who associates with bad company.''

He turned toward the door, then turned back to me. ''Monday morning. Nine o'clock. Sharp.''

The further I got from Dr. Kahn's house the better I felt. Seven dollars and eighty-seven cents is better than nothing. And he did want me to come back, so I hadn't done such a bad job after all. And it was Friday. In school, we always said TGIF, Thank God, It's Friday. In school I never really meant it, because I always liked school better than the weekends. But this summer, TGIF. I could use a couple of days off.

The lake looked delicious. Could I go for a swim now! Just thinking about it made me feel relaxed, cool water covering me like a blanket, washing the heat and aches out of my body. Maybe I'll come back at night when nobody can see me and swim. Glide through the water with long, silent strokes, like a shark. I imagined myself moving through night waters; Commander Marks leading an underwater demolition crew, closing in on the mines set to blow up the harbor in ten minutes unless we locate them and detach their fuses. Can we do it? One by one my gallant frogmen have to surface as their air tanks empty. Now I'm alone. I know how to breathe shallowly and conserve oxygen. The mines! But my tank's empty, too. Just hold your breath, Commander Marks, you can do it, big fella; all those years of swimming underwater so nobody could see you is finally going to pay off.

I was halfway home, walking along the edge of the county road, when I began to get the creepy feeling that something was following me. A little cold shiver up my spine straightened the hairs on the back of my neck. Don't turn around too fast, don't let on you know they're there. I saw a movie once where the hero pretended not to notice the bad guys creeping up on him till the last second, then he jumped behind a tree and drew his six-gun at the same time. There were no trees along the road, but plenty of rocks as big as baseballs. I timed my steps. I'd take two long ones, a short one, scoop up a rock and whirl around. I was bending over, my hand on a rock, when someone yelled, "Get him."

A car door opened and a body jumped out. I was still bent over when something hard slammed into my backside and knocked me down. I turned over with the rock in my hand. A boot came down hard on my wrist.

"Tried to put a rock through your windshield, Willie," said one of the Smith boys.

Willie Rumson strutted up. I was flat on my back and he was outlined against the pale blue sky. He looked about ten feet tall.

"Next time you pull his ladder, make sure he's still on it, Jim," said Rumson.

"Won't be a next time," said Jim. "You ain't going back to Dr. Kahn on Monday. Right?" He put both boots on my wrist.

"Answer the man, faggot," said Rumson.

"Drop dead," I said.

"You hear that?" Jim sounded almost as surprised as I was.

"I've killed better men than you for a hell of a lot less." Rumson lifted his boot over my face.

"Hold on," said Jim. "Don't stomp his face."

"Can't hurt that stomach," said Rumson.

"Just put your foot down," said Jim. "If he goes crying to Kahn and Kahn tells my dad, I'll get my head knocked off."

"Maybe I'll just kick his ribs in."

"Kick his ribs, but just a little. Don't break 'em."

Another car pulled up. I couldn't see it, but I heard its squealing brakes and felt the gravel spray from its tires on my face.

"Whatcha got there, Willie-boy?"

"A juvenile delinquent, Uncle Homer. Tried to throw that rock through my windshield."

"Let 'im up."

Jim Smith got off my wrist. A big, powerful hand grabbed my other arm and jerked me to my feet. "He's a heavy one." My face came up to his badge. He was very tall and wide. "Drop that rock, young fella."

I dropped it.

"Now why would you want to break Willie's windshield? You could cause a accident, somebody get killed." He wore the uniform of a town policeman. He had sergeant stripes on his sleeves. "Huh? What you say?"

"I . . . I didn't . . ."

"What's your name?"

"Robert Marks."

"Summer people?"

"Yes."

"Now you get on home, next time I hear about you, your folks'll have to come down to the station, pick you up. Understand?"

"Yes, sir."

"Now get going." He spun me around and booted me in the can.

I jogged all the way to the foot of my hill, and I never looked back. I heard laughter behind me.

It sounded like Willie and his Uncle Homer were sharing some big joke. About me.

Mom and Michelle looked up suddenly when I walked in. I could tell I had interrupted some deep discussion. But when Mom said "Is everything all right, Bobby?" I knew the discussion wasn't about me. If it was about me she would have looked a little guilty and offered me a snack before dinner. That was a relief. For a minute I thought maybe Homer had called her up.

"I'm going to take a little nap before dinner."

"That's fine."

"Dad be home soon?"

"No, he's tied up in the city." She bit her lower lip. "He won't be able to make it up this weekend. Business."

Michelle stared out the window.

Best news all week. Give me some time to think. Rumson, Dr. Kahn, Jim Smith, Homer; some mess. If I had to deal with my father, too, forget it.

I went into my room and I did what I always do when the going gets tough. I went to sleep. I didn't wake up until Saturday.

10

Without Dad, it was very quiet in the house. I kind of liked that. He always has something to say about everything. The weather, Mom's meals, my clothes, Michelle's makeup, an opinion for every occasion whether you ask him or not. And he's always organizing something, he just can't stand to see people lying around. Wasting your life, he calls it. Get out and do something, anything, he says. Mow the lawn, take a swim, read a book. I don't think he ever stared out the window in his life. Or had a daydream.

I just loafed around all day Saturday, looking at magazines, dozing, listening to the radio. Usually, I eat a lot on days like that, but for some reason I wasn't too hungry. My stomach muscles were still sore from all that bending. Of course, I had a few peanut butter sandwiches, and a few dishes of ice cream, but that was more for taste than for hunger. Peanut butter and ice cream are two of my favorite foods, but you've got to be careful eating them. They can hurt you. The only thing worse than a peanut butter strangle is an ice cream headache. A few times in my life I've had both at the same time, and that's murder.

They both come from eating too fast, and I'm a fast eater; you've got to get it down quick if you're afraid of being caught in the act. The peanut butter strangle hits you right away; the instant you take that first swallow and feel a lump the size of a golf ball in your throat, you know you've got it. I've tried to wash it down with cold milk or soda, even jam it down with bread crust, like you do with a fishbone, but that only makes it worse. There's nothing to do but suffer, tough it out like a man. You've got to keep swallowing, feel that golf ball move slowly down your throat until it enters your chest; it's as big as a baseball by then, shoving your heart out of the way, pressing against your breastbone, slowly, working down the alimentary canal, leaving a path of agony and destruction; as big as a softball by the time it finally falls into your stomach and lies there, heavy and hard as a cannonball, for hours, until your stomach acids slowly dissolve it.

An ice cream headache is sneakier; it takes at least a couple minutes after you swallow a too-big mouthful for the message to get back up to your brain. Torture time. Then, blam, a shot between the eyes sending you reeling against the refrigerator door, it spreads across your fore-head, a dull ache boring through your skull, you can't think, you can barely focus your eyes. Wheew. I can't get too excited about some creep standing on my wrist. I've known real pain, self-inflicted.

Saturday was painless. I could take my time eating. Michelle was down at the beach, watching Pete, and Mom was studying. She wouldn't have heard a bomb go off. But Dad has radar. No matter how quietly I open the refrigerator door, if he's somewhere in the house, when that light goes on he senses it and appears in the kitchen. Without him around, I didn't have to rush.

Michelle left right after dinner. Mom asked

her if she was seeing Pete, and when Michelle said yes, Mom just sighed. She didn't say anything else. Then she went back to her books.

I tried to read for a while, but I was so tired the words wiggled on the page. Normally, I have 20-20 vision. Once, when I was in the sixth grade and having a little trouble reading, I wore glasses for about two months. It was my mother's idea, and she got the eye doctor to go along with her. The glasses were like windowpanes, but I felt better wearing them. My real problem was the teacher, a very skinny woman who used to make fun of my weight. Well, she didn't actually make fun of me, but she always laughed when some kid in the class made a crack, like "Here come Robert Marks."

And she would say, "You must use the singular, here *comes* Robert Marks."

And the kid would say, "When you talk about Robert Marks you've got to use the plural. There's at least two of him."

And the teacher would laugh.

So I had some trouble reading, but the phoney glasses fixed it up. It was all psychological. I found out about it one night when I heard my parents arguing. My father thought it was a waste of money to get glasses when I didn't need them to help me see. After that I wouldn't wear them anymore, but my reading got better anyway.

Sunday was a draggy day. Loafing around wasn't so much fun when nobody seemed to care whether I did anything or not. Michelle was down at Marino's Beach, of course, and my mother was studying, although she seemed to be walking around the house a lot, taking breaks for tea and stepping out on the porch to stare at the lake.

Usually, we spread the Sunday newspapers around the living room, and tried to read while my father made comments about the news; but today I had all the papers to myself, and after reading Terry and The Pirates and Dick Tracy, I lost interest. I had nothing to do. By noon, I was bored.

Usually, by noon, we'd all be out of the house doing something, taking a ride through farm country or going to an auction or walking over to the community field to watch the Sunday softball game between the bachelors and the married men. The bachelors around Rumson Lake were mostly older teenagers and a few guys in their twenties who were engaged. My father sometimes played for the married men. He wasn't that great a hitter, but he was pretty good at third base; he had a really strong arm, and he never shut up the whole game—"Make 'im a hitter, chuck easy, baby, chuck easy, no hitter there, no hitter there"—and they always seemed glad to see him show up for a game. "Big Mart" they called him up at the field, even though he wasn't so big. On the way back from softball he'd go for a swim. He really liked to fill up a whole day with things to do, and he liked to have the family with him. I sort of missed him.

Around three, my mother sent me down to the beach to get Michelle. I hated that long hot walk up and down our hill. There were always battles about that walk; my father thought it was a waste of gas to drive down to the lake, and the rest of us complained that after a nice cool swim we'd get all hot again walking home. I couldn't understand why my mother didn't drive down and get Michelle herself, but the way she asked me, as if it was a great favor, and the way she looked, her mouth twitching nervously and her eyes kind of red rimmed, I didn't put up too much of a fuss.

Michelle was spread out on the sand, turning herself into a raisin, her head propped up on a beach towel so she could watch Pete show off his dives. The way he looked over at her as he walked out on the highboard, it seemed as if he was giving her a private exhibition. He was great. When he sprang off the highboard, he seemed to hang in the air for a moment, as if he was just about to take off and fly, then slowly jackknife, straighten out, and on the way down turn like a corkscrew until he went into the water as smoothly as a knife. Sometimes I felt jealous of guys who dove off the highboard, but there was no way to feel jealous of Pete, he wasn't really human, the way he looked, the things he could do; it was like watching one of those Greek gods we read about, Mercury, maybe, or Apollo.

"Mom wants you to come home now," I told Michelle.

"What for?"

"I don't know, but she's pretty upset about something."

She got right up and stuffed her things into a beach bag. "Did she say anything last night? About Pete and me?"

"We didn't talk at all."

"About anything?"

"She was studying."

"No bedside chat?" Michelle shook her head.

"Is something wrong?"

"Nothing for you to worry about," said Michelle. She waved good-bye to Pete. He waved back.

I sang, "They tried to tell us we're too young..."

"Dry up," said Michelle.

I sang, "They tried to sell us egg foo young..."

She laughed. "That's better. Now if you could only carry a tune."

By the time we got back to the house, Mom was dressed and made up, sitting at the dining room table drumming the top with a pencil.

"I'm going to need your cooperation," she said. "I'm going into the city. Right now."

"When are you coming back?" I asked.

"I'm not sure. Probably Tuesday afternoon. There's enough food in the house to tide you over, and I've left money in my jewelry box if you want to eat out. Michelle's in charge, Bobby. I'll expect you to do what she says.''

"Are you going in to see Dad?" I asked.

Mom shot Michelle a look, then said, "Of course, I'll see him. But I'm going in to get some more books I need."

Michelle asked, "Is there anything special you want us to do while you're gone?"

"Just take care of each other." She hugged us each very tightly, and then hugged us together. "I'll call you tonight when I get to the apartment."

We walked her to the car and watched her drive down the hill.

"Do you have any plans for tonight?" asked Michelle.

"I'm going to sack out early, I've got work tomorrow."

"Okay, listen. If Mom calls, and I'm not home yet, just tell her I'm asleep."

"I hate to lie," I said.

"Don't give me a hard time, you invented lying," she said.

"What if she wants to talk to you?" I asked.

"She won't if you tell her I'm asleep. She'll believe you."

"What if she insists it's very important?"

"Then put down the phone, wait a few minutes, and then tell her I'm really deeply asleep, you can't get me up."

"I don't know," I said.

"If I'm going to do favors for you, then you better be ready to return them."

"I don't know if it'll work," I said.

"Believe me, it'll work."

It worked.

11

Michelle wasn't in the house when I woke up Monday morning. She always makes her bed right away when she gets up, so I couldn't tell for sure if she came home late and left early, or never came home at all. I had my suspicions, of course.

I had breakfast, packed my lunch and went to work. Walking around the lake, it occurred to me that I had never spent a night all by myself alone in the house. I should ask her if she ever did come home last night. Then I'd know if I had been alone. It gave me the creeps to think I had been by myself.

There was only one Marino swimming around the island this morning, a red tube bobbing along behind. The swimmer's hair was very dark, so that was Vinnie. I'd heard he was studying for his law school boards this summer. Had Pete already done his laps? Or was he just too tired from last night with Michelle?

Dr. Kahn was waiting for me at the top of the driveway. Nine o'clock sharp, High Basal Time. He nodded his bald freckled head. I think that meant he was glad to see me.

"I like a boy who's punctual on Monday morning," he said. "The start of a new week. A new chance. We'll forget about last week."

"Yes, sir." I'd never forget last week.

I thought the green machine purred when I started it. You know who's the boss now, I told it. The lawn didn't look quite so big this week. My muscles started their usual complaining when I swung into my rows, but the sun baking on my back and the sweat pouring down my body felt soothing. All my blisters had broken and dried. I had a lot of dead skin on my hands, and I was getting calluses. The morning flew by. I stopped only to gas the machine and drink water.

The afternoon went more slowly. I probably shouldn't have stopped for lunch. My muscles stiffened up during the half-hour break, and it took a while to get back into the rhythm of the mowing. The sun was stronger now, it felt like the breath of a dragon on the back of my neck. When I turned and walked into the sun, the heat hit my face like a steamy towel, and I gasped for air. I didn't even have the energy to think up daydreams, I just kept marching back and forth. But by three o'clock I had cut nearly half the lawn. I thought I saw a look of surprise in Dr. Kahn's eyes when I quit for the day. I could tell he was pleased. He had nothing to say.

I went home and showered and fell asleep. It was after seven when I woke up. The house was silent and cool. Mom had stocked the refrigerator for a week, cold cuts neatly packaged and labeled, fresh fruit and vegetables, a cooked meat loaf and a cooked chicken.

I made myself a couple of chicken sandwiches with a little lettuce and gobs of mayonnaise, and a pitcher of chocolate milk, but after finishing one sandwich and two glasses of chocolate milk, I got tired of eating. The house was so quiet. I turned on the radio to keep me company, but the static was annoying. There must be a storm somewhere. So I walked down to Marino's Beach.

Pete and Michelle were nowhere in sight. Connie was cleaning up behind the snack bar counter. I couldn't see her legs, but the way she was moving I could tell she was limping. I would have asked her if she had seen Michelle, but the look she gave me was so unfriendly I just kept walking. It began to get dark, storm clouds covering the last rays of the sun. I should have turned back home right then, but I felt good walking, and I wasn't ready yet to go back to an empty house. I remembered there was a little grocery store farther down the lake toward town. It was open late. I thought I'd get an ice cream pop and a couple of candy bars for the trip back home.

It was very calm on Rumson Lake, the lull before the storm. The water barely moved. There was only one boat on the water, a sailboat, and the guy in it was paddling back to shore. The sail hung limp, like a bedsheet on a clothesline. No wind. Few cars passed. Monday night isn't exactly a jumping night on Rumson Lake. Everybody's recovering from the weekend.

The man in the grocery store seemed glad to see me, there was nobody else in the store. He put down the newspaper he was reading. "That Mickey Mantle, he's gonna be a great one," he said. "Who you like better, Mantle or Mays?"

"Mantle," I said. I could tell that's what he wanted to hear.

"Sure. When the going gets tough, down to the wire, you can't trust the colored. They choke."

I paid for my ice cream and candy bars and got out of there as quick as I could. I didn't want to get into an argument with the guy. The ice cream tasted watery. Crummy ice cream. The pop was misshapen, as if it had thawed and been refrozen a couple of times. I ate it fast to get it over with, and started on the first candy bar. It was too soft and gooey.

I should have started an argument. Can't trust the colored. Like Jackie Robinson and Larry Doby? That would have stopped him cold. And then I remembered that Willie Mays had just gone into the Army. If Mickey Mantle's so great, how come he can't even pass an Army physical?

I felt disgusted with myself. Why'd I let him get away with saying that? By not saying anything, I let him think that I agreed with him.

Maybe he was just testing me, now he thinks I'm one of those anti-Negro creeps.

If my father was there, you would have heard an argument all right. He doesn't let remarks like that pass by. I wondered what Pete would have said. I started getting angrier and angrier. I turned around to go back to the grocery store, at least to tell the guy his ice cream stinks, but then I turned around again. Coward. Talk about being a rug. Everybody walks all over me. And laughs about it. My whole body shook, I was filled with angry energy. I kicked a beer can out of my way, and it skittered across the county road. A car coming along stopped short, then made a screaming U-turn. It was a blue-and-white Chevrolet. Willie Rumson jumped out.

"You've had the course, faggot."

"Take a hike, Rummie."

We just stared at each other for a few seconds. We were both shocked.

"What you say?"

"You heard me, Rummie. Take a hike."

He took a step backward, then turned toward his car. I had a wonderful feeling. He's retreating. He's just a bully and when I called his bluff he was through. But then he crooked his finger toward the car, and his hoods came out, two girls and three guys. One of them was Jim Smith.

"Now you gonna tell me not to stomp his face, Jim? What if that beer can went through the window, hit me, and I went into the lake. Huh?"

"Okay, okay, rap 'im a couple and let's get going."

"He tried to kill me. The second time."

"C'mon, Willie." Jim put his hand on one of Willie's wide, skinny shoulders. Willie shook it off.

"I'm gonna teach this fat slob a lesson once and for all."

"Just make it fast," said Jim.

Rumson snapped his fingers. "Take him, boys." Like a movie. The two other guys ran over and each of them grabbed one of my arms. I struggled, but they had firm grips. Rumson sauntered up like Al Capone. I got a little scared. He must be crazy. Why else would a guy with such a good skinny body have to pick on me?

"This is it, fats. Kiss tomorrow good-bye."

"C'mon, Willie, just hit him and get it over with."

Willie screamed, "If you got no guts, Jim, just move out."

Jim came over to me. "Listen, fatty, I've got nothing to do with this. You understand?"

"Move out!"

Jim shrugged and walked away. I was sorry to see him go. We all watched him slouch down the county road until he was just another gray shadow in the dusk. When Rumson turned back to me, his thin face was twisted, and a vein as thick as a telephone cord stood out in the middle of his forehead.

"Your ass is grass, faggot, and I'm the lawn mower."

He took one step toward me, his fists clenched. I kicked him right in the groin. Well, almost. I had seen it in a movie once, the hero being held by two outlaws while the leader came at him with a branding iron. I sagged back against the guys holding my arms, and when I felt them tighten their grips to support my weight, I aimed my right foot at the fly of Rumson's fatigue pants. He was very quick. He half-turned while my foot was in midair, and caught most of my kick on his hip. It still had enough force to drive him back a few steps. If I had connected he'd have never gotten up.

He was smiling now, he didn't look angry at all. "Waal, we're gonna see just how tough you are with a tire jack wrapped around your head." He snapped his fingers at one of the girls. "Laurie. Get the jack out of the trunk."

"Not me, Willie." She was thin, kind of pretty, with a lot of makeup. She looked closer to my age than Rumson's. "I'm not going to jail for killing that slob."

"You don't do what I tell you, you'll wish you were in jail."

"What's the big deal? You're gonna kill somebody for kicking a beer can?" said Laurie.

"You don't understand anything." That vein was pumping hard. "Fat faggots come up from the city, smartass Jews and Wops and Greeks, always making deals, looking to cheat real Americans out of everything. Laughing at us all the way to the bank. Get away with anything, huh, take a man's job, take his land, take his house."

"C'mon, Willie." One of the guys holding me

laughed nervously. "This meatball couldn't even take a leak without someone giving him a hand."

"He took my job," screamed Rumson. "My job! And I served! In the Corps!"

"You'll get a job."

"And his father took my lake away."

"That's crazy," said Laurie.

"Crazy, huh? Get that tire jack."

"Look, Willie." She was shaking. "You hurt him bad, even Homer won't help you."

The other girl stepped out of the shadows. She would have been very pretty except for the scars around her mouth, thin red scars. An auto accident, I thought, she must have smashed her face against the windshield. When she talked I could see she was missing her side teeth, and her front ones were too white and perfect to be real. "I got a better idea, Willie."

"Talk fast, Annie."

"You want to get rid of him, right? Destroy him?"

"Yeah."

"You beat him to a pulp, so what? Everybody knows you can take anybody on the lake."

"What's your idea?"

"Really destroy him. So bad he can't ever show his face around here again."

"Yeah?" Rumson looked interested.

"Strip him naked and leave him on the road."

Rumson slapped his leg and began cackling. Laurie gave Annie a relieved look, and Annie rolled her eyes. The guys holding my arms loosened their grips. "Great, Willie," said one of them, "that's really great."

I broke loose and ran. I flew. I never moved so fast in my life. Right down the middle of the county road, arms pumping, legs like pistons. Once, I glanced over my shoulder. Rumson and his gang were gone.

I'm going to make it. Around the next bend in the road, the hill to my house. Once I hit the hill I'll be safe, even if they follow me up I can run into any house on the hill. I'm going to make it, just a little farther, I feel a second wind, new energy, just a few more steps.

A car coming toward me slowed. Maybe Pete, someone who knew me. The car stopped, doors flew open, and Rumson's two hoods had me by the arms again and were dragging me into the car. I tried to break loose again, but I had no strength left. They shoved me into the back of the car. Rumson, at the wheel, was cackling.

"You can't get away from me, faggot, I know these roads like the palm of my hand." He was bouncing on the driver's seat, and the car was swerving.

"For Christ's sake, take it easy," yelled Annie.

"Eddie. Blindfold him."

"What?" One of the guys holding me down in the back leaned forward.

"Wrap something around his eyes, a handkerchief or something."

"What for?"

"Just do it."

Eddie found a greasy rag on the ledge behind our seat and tied it over my eyes.

"Where you going?" asked Laurie.

"You'll see. But he won't." Rumson's cackle was beginning to echo in my stomach. "Now everybody shut up. We're going for a little ride."

I settled back in the seat. Got to think. I'm in a movie. Or a daydream. We're going for a little ride. How many times had I heard that line? Figure out where I am, the hero always does that. Right turn. Left turn. Down a hill. U-turn. Forget it. I'd be lost now even if I could see where we were going.

Listen for clues. Once, in a spy movie, the hero was blindfolded, but he remembered hearing a creaking sound and later he figured out he was near windmills in Holland. But all I could hear was the screaming of tires as Rumson made two-wheel turns, and the heavy breathing inside the car. Mostly my own.

I was scared but I wasn't petrified. My mind was working. They weren't going to kill me. Rumson wasn't that crazy. Probably dump me somewhere on a country road. It would be a long walk back, but I'd make it. Unless they really stripped me naked. They wouldn't do that. Would they? Now I started to feel petrified.

We drove for a long time, more hills, more sharp turns. Too many. He must be doubling back to make me think we were very far away. The car jerked to a stop.

"Everybody out."

The ground was mushy.

"Put him in the middle."

They pushed me forward. I sank up to my ankles in soft mud.

"Step up, fats."

I lifted my leg and somebody shoved me forward. I fell down against wet wood that began to sway under me. A boat. I heard the others climb in.

"Shove off, Eddie."

"Jesus, we're stuck. He must weigh a ton."

"C'mon, push. Push!"

The boat rocked, there was a scraping sound, and then we were floating on the water. The boat nearly tipped as Eddie climbed in. He dripped water all over me. I tried to sit up, but somebody pushed me down.

"Okay, me hearties, put your backs into it." Rumson playing Captain Kidd. "Shall we make him walk the plank?"

"It's starting to rain," said Annie. "There's too many of us in this boat."

"There'll be one less coming back," said Rumson. "Now shut up."

The raindrops were big and cold. I started to shiver. My teeth chattered.

"Look at him," said Laurie. "Willie, this is crazy.

I bit down hard on my lip. Not going to get any satisfaction from me.

They rowed for a long time. I thought about ripping the rag off my eyes, but I didn't want to do anything to get Rumson crazy mad. I thought about jumping out of the boat, but it was dark and I didn't know where we were.

After a while the boat scraped bottom. They pulled me out and walked me through knee-high water to land.

"Laurie, Annie. Strip him."

"Do it yourself."

"It was your idea. Strip him or I'll drown him."

I felt a hand on my belt buckle. "NO." I turned and tried to run. Someone tripped me, and they were suddenly all on top of me, laughing, pulling at my clothes. All I could think of was that they would see me naked, without any clothes, stark naked, and I turned and twisted, flailed my arms, kicked, punched, bit. I was a wild man and every time I heard a shout or a groan, when I knew I got one of them, I had new strength. But it didn't last too long. Someone was sitting on my head, there was someone holding each arm and leg, and I could feel and hear my clothes being pulled off my body. Shoes, pants, shirt, underwear.

"On your feet." Somebody helped me up. "Now listen, fats. You just bend over and hold your ankles..."

"He can't get down that far."

"Jesus."

"Okay, then. Your knees. That's it. Just stay like that. If you move, just so much as move, I'm coming back with a sharp stick and guess where I'm going to put it."

I held my knees. I felt my buttocks quivering. I could imagine them jiggling and shaking. I wondered how dark it was.

"Don't move now." Footsteps moving away. "Not so much as a blink." Rumson's voice was getting farther and farther away. The boat creaked. They must be getting into it. Oars squeaked in the oarlocks.

"Don't move." He was shouting, but I could tell his voice was coming from a distance.

"Lookit that can," said Eddie.

"Two moons tonight," said Annie, and their laughter echoed and re-echoed over the water.

When it died away I stood up and took off the blindfold. I was alone on the island in the middle of Rumson Lake. I fell down on my hands and knees and cried, and I didn't feel the rain until the night exploded with thunder and lightning and the wind drove nails of rain into my naked body.

12

I am going to die.

I am sinking into the island. My hands and knees are in mud puddles rising to drown me. Soon the water will reach my belly. The wind-whipped rain streams off my back. Soon it will rise to my chest and I will sink to meet it, my mouth and nose submerged in muddy water that will fill my lungs and kill me.

Poor fat Bobby Marks. One fat joke. Better if they never find my body. I don't want to be caught dead with my clothes off.

I shiver as the water touches my stomach, a bloated hammock swaying beneath me. In a little while it'll all be over.

The water reaches my elbows, laps at my backside.

They'll be sorry. Dad and Mom and Michelle and Joanie and Pete and Dr. Kahn and Connie and Homer and the man in the grocery store and even Jim Smith and Eddie and Laurie and Annie. Maybe even Willie Rumson.

Poor fat Bobby Marks. We knew he was a slob and a fat pig and a laughingstock, but we didn't want him to die for that. It was just a joke. Like him.

The water feels warmer now, it's up to my shoulders. It covers my back like a blanket. Just a few minutes more.

Serves me right. Should have been a junior counselor taking care of little kids, let them make fun of me, that's all I'm good for. Serves me right. Who did I think I was? Big shot. Lie about my age to get a job. Wasn't even my own idea. Joanie made me do it. Just walk all over Bobby Marks like a rug, push him around like a beach ball, jerk him up and down like a Yo-Yo. Always making up stories about heroes because you're nothing yourself. Nothing but a nothing, nothing but a fat, ugly, hanging bag of flab, disgusting; they won't be sorry when they find your body, they'll just laugh their heads off.

What's a dead whale doing in Rumson Lake, they'll ask.

Crybaby. Slob. Fat nothing. Better off dead.

"On your feet, Marks."

I looked around. I saw no one in the darkness.

"Stand up."

The voice was familiar.

"Up. Get up."

Lightning hit the water, the black sky parted like curtains at high noon, flooding the island with light. But there was no one there.

"I SAID GET UP. YOU CAN DO IT, BIG FELLA."

The water touched my lips. Be so easy now to relax into the soft mud, get it over with.

"ON YOUR FEET. YOU'RE NOT GONNA LET THOSE BASTARDS KILL YOU. YOU BEAT THE LAWN, YOU CAN BEAT THEM. YOU'RE TOUGH. YOU RAN, YOU FOUGHT, YOU'LL DO IT AGAIN. YOU'LL DO IT TILL YOU WIN."

I recognized the voice.

Captain Marks, Commander Marks, Big Bob Marks.

It was me.

I stood up.

There were wet, sucking sounds as I pulled my arms out of the mud, as I stumbled up to higher, drier ground. I waited for the next streak of lightning to look around. The old cabin. I ran toward it, ignoring the stones and branches cutting my bare feet. I smashed the door open with my shoulder and fell in.

The roof leaked, but it was warmer and drier inside. The floor of the cabin was covered with damp mattresses. I nearly tripped over an empty beer bottle. Lightning showed me dozens of beer cans, piles of food wrappers, a broken whiskey bottle, what looked like old white balloons, cigarette butts, a pair of panties. Make-out island.

I collapsed on one of the mattresses. I'd be safe here for a while. No one would be coming out tonight. Rest for a few minutes, then make a plan for escape. The lightning and thunder sounded farther away now, the storm was passing. The steady rain drumming on the roof put me to sleep.

Birds woke me. It was still dark. The rain had stopped. Be dawn soon. Got to get moving before the light. If only I had some clothes. I felt around the cabin. The panties tore when I pulled them on. I found part of a filthy old sheet and wrapped it around myself. I stepped out of the cabin.

The air was thick and sweet on the island. Wet leaves brushed against me. Small animals scurried out of my way. I thought of snakes. Did rattlers always give warning? But copperheads and water moccasins never did.

I walked to the water's edge. It was getting lighter now, but mist rolled along the surface of the lake. I heard the splash of a paddle, and saw a blurred light moving toward me. Was it Rumson coming back?

"Are you okay?"

"Who is it?"

"Jim Smith." A canoe bumped up on the shore.

"What do you want?"

"I heard about what happened. I'll take you back." He jumped out of the canoe and pulled it up on shore.

"I don't need your help."

"How you gonna get back?"

"I'll swim back."

"Sure. Get a cramp, or get bit by a moccasin. C'mon, hurry up."

He flashed his light on my clothes, neatly folded on the front seat of the canoe. "I found them by the old dock. Get dressed. Make it snappy."

Except for one sock, everything was there. Even my wallet. I dressed and climbed into the canoe. He shoved off and jumped in. The canoe moved silently, swiftly, over the water. The sky began to glow with pink. We were halfway back to my side of the lake before I could see his face. He looked very serious.

"Why'd you come to get me?"

"I don't give a damn about you, kid, but Willie's got enough problems."

The canoe glided alongside a dock near my hill. "Okay, fats, do yourself a favor. Just forget about tonight. Now get going."

I scrambled up on the dock. By the time I turned around he was paddling away, long, powerful strokes that sent the canoe shooting over the water. Jim Smith never looked back.

I trudged up the hill. Except for the driver of a milk truck, no one saw me. The house was still.

I peeked into Michelle's room. Her bed was empty. I took a shower, and made myself breakfast. Scrambled eggs and bacon and toast with butter and jelly. I was still hungry. I found the other chicken sandwich from last night. I drank the rest of the chocolate milk, out of the pitcher.

The phone rang. The sound of it scared me. I let it ring a few times before I got up the nerve to pick it up. What now?

"Hello?"

"Oh, Bobby, thank God. I was so worried. Where were you last night, I called and called."

"I didn't hear the phone ring, Mom." That was no lie.

"It must have been the storm. Is everything all right? Is Michelle there?"

"She's not up yet." That was no lie, either. "When are you coming back?"

"This afternoon. Anything new?"

"No."

"What've you been doing?"

"Nothing much."

"Were you scared during the storm?"

"Just a little thunder and lightning, that's all."

She laughed. "Well, I feel a lot better now, believe me. Give my love to Michelle. I'll see you later."

I felt good, not at all tired. I cleaned up my dirty dishes, packed my lunch, and listened to the radio till eight. Might as well get an early start today, knock off the rest of that lawn.

I met Michelle coming up the hill. She looked terrible, her hair all stringy, her clothes muddy and damp.

"What a night," she said. "Pete's truck got stuck in the mud, and then he got a flat . . . Did Mom call?"

"I told her you weren't up yet. She's coming back this afternoon."

"Were you home during the storm?" she asked.

"No, I was on make-out island."

"I don't think that's funny. I better hurry up or I'll be late." She took two steps up the hill, then turned. "Bob? Thanks a lot. I really appreciate this."

I sang, "Any Time . . ."

She laughed. Made her look a lot better. She's really pretty, if you like that type.

I skipped down the hill, and I might have trotted all the way to Dr. Kahn's if I hadn't figured I might need my strength later on. You never know what's going to happen on Rumson Lake.

13

Tiredness hit me like a ton of bricks in the afternoon. My legs got wobbly, and twice I had to go back over a row to cut grass I had missed. The lawn began to rise and fall like the deck of an ocean liner in a storm. Or a rowboat on Rumson Lake. It was better when I closed my eyes, but then I'd start missing grass again. I kept plowing along, and I finished the lawn by three o'clock.

The walk home seemed much farther than usual. The county road was undulating like the lawn. I had to step carefully because I couldn't focus on the concrete; sometimes it seemed to rise up at me, sometimes it seemed to fall away. I kept looking for Rumson's Chevy. I got myself up the hill by pretending I was ascending Mount

Everest hand over hand on a rope. That's what it felt like anyway.

Right to bed. Sometime toward evening, I felt someone pulling off my shoes and pants. It was my mother. She was smiling.

The rest of that week I was nervous. But it was an exciting kind of nervousness, butterflies, sighing breaths. I couldn't sit still too long, and I wasn't very hungry. My mother noticed it at dinner Wednesday night.

"You've got ants in your pants," she said.

"I'm okay."

She peered at me over the table. "You look a little peaked."

"I feel fine."

"Are the Marinos working you too hard?"

Michelle almost choked on her corn.

"You might be getting a little too much sun, Bobby, your face is very tanned. Are you wearing a hat?"

"Yeah."

"I think I'll stop by the beach tomorrow. I'd like to see what they're having you do."

"You shouldn't do that, Mom," said Michelle. "It makes him seem like a baby."

"He is my baby."

"See, that's what I mean," said Michelle.

"You don't look too well yourself," said Mom. "Those black circles under your eyes."

"Those brats are running me ragged," said Michelle. "I can't wait for college to start, I need a vacation."

"Now that you mention it, we've got to start thinking about clothes for school. I don't want to leave it to the last minute. When are we going to sit down and make that list?"

They started talking about college clothes, and Michelle and I exchanged looks. That was a close one. After dinner, when Mom went to study, Michelle came in to help me with the dishes.

"Don't you have a date tonight?"

"It's Pete's birthday, the whole family's going out to dinner."

"How come you're not going?"

"They're not too crazy about us going together, so we thought it would be better if I didn't come."

"Why?"

"I don't know. Pete says they're worried about

him finishing college, he's not such a great student. But I think it's something else and he doesn't want to hurt my feelings. It'd be different if my name were Marko instead of Marks. Understand?''

"That's stupid. Look at what happened to Romeo and Juliet, and they were both Italian.''

"Pardon me if I don't laugh.''

"Did Mom say anything about Dad?''

"I think he's coming up next weekend. I talked to her last night and she said going into the city was the best thing she ever did.''

"Do you think something is wrong?''

"Everybody's got problems,'' said Michelle.

"No, I mean, like are they going to get a divorce or something?''

"How's your job going?''

"Are you going to treat me like a baby, too?''

"I just don't think I should discuss it with you.''

"Everybody's got secrets this summer.''

"You should talk.''

Still no sign of Rumson on Thursday. Dr. Kahn had me spend the day clearing and widening the drainage ditch along the county road, and I kept expecting Rumson to drive up anytime. I had a pick and a shovel, and I would have used them if he'd tried anything. Butterflies all day, but I didn't really mind them. Usually when I'm nervous it's because I know something's going to happen to embarrass me. Like getting weighed in front of the class, or not picked to play on a team, or having to chin or climb a rope in front of all the guys in the gym. That kind of nervousness feels like a cold stone in my stomach. But this was different. It was the same kind of butterflies I'd read about when an actor is waiting for the opening night curtain or the heavyweight champ is waiting for the opening bell before a fight. A light fluffy nervousness that disappears after the actor says his first line or the champ throws his first punch. On edge. Ready to go. I tried to think about it, but I didn't get very far. I knew it had something to do with that night on the island. Something had happened to me, and it wasn't all bad, not at all.

Joanie called me Thursday night. Person-to-person from the city. I never had a person-to-person long distance call before. The connection wasn't too good.

"Bob?"

"Yeah?"

"It's Joanie."

"Hi."

"Hi, yourself. Have you been thinking about me?" It was her voice all right, but she sounded sort of teasey, not like her at all.

"Sure," I lied.

"I'm coming up Saturday."

"That's great."

"I'm just giving you a little advance warning."

"How come?"

She started giggling. "I don't want you to have a heart attack."

"Because you're coming up?"

"You'll see what I mean. Just be prepared."

"For what?" I asked.

"Curiosity killed the..."

"We went through that already. Were you in the hospital?"

"Yes," she said.

"Did you have an operation?"

"Yes. Is this twenty questions?"

"Are you all right now?"

"Better than ever," she said.

"Was your life in danger? Is that why you needed an operation?"

"No, I wanted the operation."

There was a few seconds of silence on the line while I tried to think. I had a thought that made me a little sick.

"Bob? You still there?"

"Joanie? Did you ... did you ... have something removed?"

"Who told you that?" Her voice got sharp.

"Nobody. Joanie ... were you ... were you ... in trouble?"

"BOB!" The receiver banged against my ear. "What's wrong with you?"

I felt better. "If you're going to be so secretive ..."

"You'll just have to wait till Saturday. What've you been doing?"

My mother was in the room so I couldn't tell her. "Oh, nothing much."

"We'll be able to start the project soon."

"Okay."

"You don't sound too enthusiastic."

"I might be dead after I see you."

She giggled again. "That's true."

The operator cut in. "Your three minutes are up. Please signal when you're finished."

"Got to go now. See you Saturday."

"Bye." I waited for her to hang up.

"Hang up," she said.

"You hang up." I tapped the receiver against the side of the phone.

"That's an old trick," she said.

"You're the tricky one."

She laughed and hung up.

My mother said, "Was that Joanie?" As if she hadn't been eavesdropping.

"No, it was Ike. He wanted to know if I liked him."

"What did she say?"

"She's coming up Saturday."

"Is that all?"

"Well, there was something else, but I can't tell you. She swore me to secrecy. She told me all about her operation, but I can't tell you."

"Oh?" I could tell my mother was trying very hard not to laugh. "Bobby, you're going to have to get up very early in the morning to put one over on your mother."

"So you do know. And you won't tell me."

"My lips are sealed." She pretended she was zippering her lips. "You'll find out Saturday."

I put on a German accent. "Ve haff vays of getting information out of you Amedicans."

"Not the Breyers ice cream torture, anything but that." Her eyes got very wide and she crossed her hands over her heart.

"Das iss rrright. A gallon uff cherry vanilla, vun inch out uff your reach, und if you don't tell me ze truth before it melts...kissss tomorrow goot-bye."

Mom laughed. It sounded nice. I hadn't heard her laugh in a while. "You win. The ice cream, that is. I just happened to have picked up a quart on the way home."

"Maybe later," I said. She looked surprised. I love Breyers ice cream, but I just didn't feel like eating. I was thinking about tomorrow, Friday, the day the Smiths showed up.

I got the feeling Jim Smith avoided me all Friday morning. Even when we worked near each other, he kept looking away. His brother had a few wise things to say to me, but Jim was quiet. When I went up the ladder to check the gutters, Jim grabbed his brother's arm and pulled him around the house to one of the side flower beds. We didn't talk until his father was collecting their money from Dr. Kahn and his brother was loading the truck.

"You say anything to anybody?" he asked. He was rolling the garden hose and he didn't look at me.

"Not yet."

He glanced up at that. "You know what's going to happen if you say one word?"

"As long as Rummie stays off my back you've got nothing to worry about." It sounded terrific. I couldn't remember which movie I got it from.

"Willie's out of town."

"Where'd he go?"

"None of your business." Then Jim shrugged. "He's not so bad. You got to understand him. He came back the next morning to get you off the island. When he couldn't find you, he got scared and went upstate to visit one of his brothers. He thought you drowned."

"You didn't tell him?"

"No."

"You afraid what he'd do to you?"

Jim shook his head. "Just wanted to give him a chance to cool off. He's not a bad guy, he's just had some problems." He dropped the hose at my feet and trotted off to the truck.

Talk about secrets. I've got a secret, and Joanie's got a secret, and Michelle's got a secret, probably Mom and Dad, too, and Jim Smith's got a secret from Willie Rumson, who probably had secrets, too. If I ever get to be an author, I'll write a book called *The Secret Summer*. Two hundred pages, all of them blank except the last page, where I'll write, Sorry, folks, the whole story's a big secret.

At three o'clock I went up to the porch. Dr. Kahn was sitting in a rocking chair, his little leather purse on his lap. He began counting out money. "I like a boy who improves," he said. "You've still got a long way to go, however." He counted out twelve dollars and seventy-five cents into my hand. "Monday, morning. Nine o'clock sharp."

"Have a nice weekend, Dr. Kahn." I really meant it, I felt so good about my talk with Jim Smith and the compliment from the evil Dr. K. So good that I was halfway around the lake before I figured out that the doctor of mathematics had cheated me out of a dollar. Thirty hours at fifty cents an hour was fifteen dollars, minus five half-hour lunch breaks at twenty-five cents each was $13.75, not $12.75.

Okay this time. But nobody pulls a fast one on Big Bob twice.

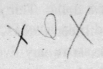

14

Dad was quiet at dinner Friday night. When he did talk, he was very polite, like a guest in the house. He complimented Mom on her roast beef, even though it wasn't as well done as he liked it, and on the vegetables, which were soggy from cooking too long. Mom smiled a lot and patted his shoulder. When Michelle left for her date, Dad wished her a nice time. He didn't seem to notice how tight her dress was. He asked me how things were going, but before I had a chance to answer he started talking about the weather, how hot and dry it was after last week's storm. I felt like a fish who got off the hook. I didn't want to tell him about Dr. Kahn yet, and I didn't want to get into a pack of lies about working around Marino's Beach. I couldn't tell if Dad just didn't care anymore, or if he had a lot of his own problems on his mind, or if he just didn't want to get involved right now. Pick one, two or three. Or all of the above.

I started to clear the table, my night again, but he waved me off.

"We'll take care of it." He pulled out his wallet. "Would you like to take the bus into town? See a movie? I'll pick you up afterward."

Very strange behavior. He was usually such a cheapskate. He was trying to get rid of me.

"No, thanks. I feel like reading in bed."

"Suit yourself."

Mom nodded me out of the room. I couldn't leave fast enough for them.

I slammed my door, then quietly opened it a crack. An old spy trick. I missed a lot of their conversation because they were running water in the kitchen sink, but I heard enough.

"I just don't think it's fair to the kids," he said.

"Michelle won't be around and Bobby'll be very busy in the tenth grade."

"But they need to know someone's there for them."

"Even after I start teaching regularly, I'll be home soon after Bobby..."

"These things just don't work out, Lenore."

"They do if people want..." The rest of what she said got lost in the clatter of dishes, and so did his answer.

"...and you could go in with Fred. He's been after you for years," she said.

"Miller isn't giving anything away," said Dad. "I'd have to take a twenty percent cut in pay, and no security."

"But that's the point. It wouldn't matter. I'd be taking up the slack, and you'd be free to do what you've always wanted to do. Quit Allied and take a gamble. At least that's what you've always said you really wanted."

"When I'm ready. After the kids are out of college."

"That's at least another seven years," she said.

"By then you'll be Superintendent of Schools. I'll be able to retire." He laughed, but it was a nasty laugh that sounded as if it came out of his nose instead of his mouth.

"Marty, if my working is going to come

between us I'll stop studying right now. I'd much rather spend the summer in the garden and down at the beach. I'll just forget the whole thing.''

"Sure. And I'll have to spend the rest of my life hearing how I kept you from working."

"I'll never say another word."

"That'll be the day." He stomped out of the kitchen. From the sound of his footsteps I figured he was going out on the porch.

Mom finished the dishes, took out the garbage and slammed the kitchen cabinets shut. The kitchen lights clicked off. When I heard her footsteps coming toward my bedroom, I jumped into bed with my clothes on, and pulled the top sheet up to my chin. She must have stood in the doorway a long time, because it seemed like ten minutes between the sounds of my door opening and closing.

I got out of bed and undressed. So that's the big problem. Dad doesn't want Mom working. Michelle was right. But Dad never seemed to mind when Mom took courses or did volunteer charity work with poor kids. Sometimes, when I was younger, I got a little jealous when she talked about kids she was helping out, teaching them to read or taking them on trips, but after a while I started feeling very proud of her. I thought Dad did, too. At least he said he did.

When Mom was a volunteer teacher in Harlem she would tell us stories at dinner about really tough kids who carried knives to school and got into serious trouble with the police, stealing cars and mugging old ladies. Good stories. I filed them away for when I'd be a writer.

Once, we brought one of the kids up for a weekend. His name was Bill Witherspoon. He was couple of years older than me, and very nice. He wanted to be a boxer. He showed me how to throw a left jab, and how to protect your kidneys in a clinch.

We all went down to the lake one afternoon and everyone stared at Bill, and shook their heads and grumbled when he went into the water. While he was having a diving contest with Michelle, Mr. Marino came over to my parents.

"Hey, Marty, you know better than this," he said.

"Better than what, Vincent?"

"I don't care for myself, I got friends in all walks of life. But this is a family beach."

"So go enjoy it." My father's voice got hard.

"Marty, we own property here. You want to have something you can leave Bobby, right?"

"Like how to be a bigot?"

Mr. Marino pointed a finger at my father. "I don't like your tone of voice."

My father stood up. "Maybe you want to try and change it."

My mother got right in between them. "That boy is a weekend guest, Vincent. And this isn't like you at all."

Mr. Marino spread his hands. "Believe me, Lenore, I'm not prejudiced. I'm thinking about my kids." He nodded toward Bill Witherspoon. "It's not all their fault, but colored people bring more colored people, and that's the end of a place."

"You finished, Vincent?" asked my father.

"Enough said, Lenore." Mr. Marino took one of my mother's hands in both of his, and patted it. "No hard feelings. You understand."

"See you tomorrow, Vincent," said my father. "On the beach."

It rained the next day, so we all ate out and went to the movies in Grantsville, which is about twenty miles from Rumson Lake, and has some Negroes living in the town. We never talked about it again, but Mom didn't bring up any more charity kids after that.

I hung around Saturday. Mom played records, just to break up the silence, I think. She fooled around in the garden, but I could tell she didn't care if the flowers grew or not. Dad was in and out. He went to a golf driving range with one of the neighbors and then he went swimming. Michelle was down at the beach.

It was like a morgue at dinner. The chicken was burnt, but my father didn't say a word. He didn't even shoot me a dirty look when I sucked on my drumstick. That's one of his pet peeves, noisy eating. I could've slurped soup that night or crunched an ice cube and I don't think he would have opened his mouth. Michelle peeled sunburned skin off her arm, right at the table. Normally, that would have driven him wild. Nothing. The only sound was Mom putting plates

156

down. She managed to rattle the table every time. I think she did it purposely.

Michelle asked me to do the dishes for her; she had a date. She said she'd pay me back during the week. I said okay.

"We're going to the Millers', Michelle," said Mom. "They're expecting you, too. You knew that."

"I have something better to do."

"I don't think that's right. Joanie will be very disappointed."

"I do not want to go. Period."

"Marty?" My mother was appealing for a decision.

Dad just shrugged and left the table.

"Do what you want, Michelle," said my mother.

We got to the Millers' about eight-thirty. Mr. and Mrs. Miller were waiting at the door, grinning like monkeys. They couldn't stand still they were so excited. Joanie was standing in the middle of the living room, her back to us.

"Da dum," said Mr. Miller, waving his arm with a flourish.

Joanie turned around.

At first, I saw only her eyes. They were both black, like she had been in a fight. Two black eyes.

"Gorgeous," shrieked my mother, rushing over to hug Joanie.

"Congratulations," said my father. He shook Mr. Miller's hand. "A very nice job."

"We got the best plastic surgeon in the city," said Mrs. Miller.

My mother let Joanie loose and stepped back to look at her. "Darling, you are beautiful."

And then I saw it.

Her nose was gone.

"Well?" Joanie was smiling at me. She looked horrible. Her face was puffy and bruised. Her new little nose was red and scaly.

"It looks great," I said.

Mr. Miller was pouring drinks for my parents. Over his shoulder, he said, "There's Coke and ice cream in the fridge, why don't you kids help yourself."

We went into the kitchen. Joanie scooped out a huge chunk of ice cream for me, and a much smaller one for herself. We sat down at the kitchen table. I felt like I was with a stranger.

"Did it hurt?"

"I didn't feel anything during the operation. It hurt a little afterwards, but not much. Now it feels funny sometimes, like my skin is very tight there, but that'll go away."

"It's a nice nose." I really sounded dumb.

"We picked it out from photographs."

"The doctor just . . . chopped it off?"

"With a chisel. Like a sculptor."

"It's really very nice." I hated looking at it, but I couldn't take my eyes off it.

"We really should have waited until the swelling goes down, but that won't be for another couple of weeks. I couldn't wait for you to see it. Was it a complete surprise? Did you suspect anything?"

"No, I didn't . . ."

"I can't believe it myself. When I see myself in a mirror, I can't believe it's really me."

"Did you plan it for a long time?"

"It was really my mother's idea."

For some reason, that made me feel a little better. I ate my first spoonful of ice cream.

"You can't have it done until your nose stops

growing, but we've been talking about it for a couple of years.''

"You never told me."

"What was there to talk about?"

"I mean, such a big thing, and we talked about everything else."

"I wanted it to be a surprise."

"Joanie? Why'd you do it?"

"Surprise you?"

"No, get a nose job."

She looked at me as if I was crazy. "Because it was so ugly. I hated it. Couldn't you tell? I hated to go to school, I hated to go out on the street, I hated the way people stared at me."

"I never stared at you."

"I know. That's why I wanted to surprise you."

"It really looks nice."

"What've you been doing?" she asked.

"Not too much." I didn't feel like telling her all the things that had happened. I felt she was different, and that she wouldn't understand.

"We're going back into the city for the week, but then I'll be back for good. We can start our project if you still want to."

"Okay."

Her father called, "Joanie, come in here for a minute."

While she was gone, I gobbled down the ice cream, just shoveled in the spoonfuls as fast as I could. I knew exactly what was going to happen and I didn't care. Blam, that shot between the eyes, and a dull ache boring through the skull, my old ice cream headache pal.

15

I always used to think of summers in slow motion. I hated them and thought they would never end. I'd be chugging along through the fall and the winter, enjoying school during the week, enjoying weekends and holidays at Rumson Lake, walking alone in the snow or reading in front of the fireplace or kidding around with Joanie, and then spring would come. Everybody else got excited when the first green shoots came up through the cold ground and the air lost its bite, but I'd start worrying about the summer. That bottomless hole in my year. No way to avoid it; I would stumble and begin falling, slowly, end over end, for two months that went on forever, waiting to crash back into the autumn again, like a bad dream that wakes you up in the middle of the night covered by sweat, with a cold lump in your stomach.

But this summer was spinning along. I lost track of days. I'd wake up before the alarm clock and stretch the stiffness out of my arms and legs and back. Every morning I woke up sore, but it was getting easier and easier to get out of bed. I started touching my toes a few times to work out the kinks in my back. I could actually touch my toes. By the time I was on the county road I felt loose, like all my joints were oiled and greased. I couldn't wait to get at that lawn. My blisters were gone. I had tough yellow calluses in their place. I rarely thought about Willie Rumson.

Dad came up the next weekend, but it was as if he wasn't there. He played softball, tennis, he went swimming; he kept himself busy the whole weekend. I saw him only at meals. We hardly talked. I had decided to tell him about my job, but it just never came up. The closest was Saturday night at dinner when he suddenly said, ''I hear you're keeping yourself pretty busy.''

''Yeah.'' I started getting the story together in my mind, so I wouldn't have to tell him I had lied in the beginning, but he didn't give me a chance to talk.

"Your mother says you get home really tired. That's good. Pete Marino keeps you hopping."

Michelle started talking with her mouth full. "So much to do at that place." She flashed me a shut up look. "But I'd trade jobs in a minute. Yesterday a six-year-old boy went into the woods with a marshmallow and a book of matches and tried to start a campfire. He almost burned the whole place down."

That changed the subject, and they talked for a few minutes about Michelle's camp job. On her way out that night she gave me a wink.

I didn't talk to Mom much either. She was studying again, harder than ever, reading books, taking notes, making charts and lists. By the time I got up for breakfast, she had already finished hers and was at her desk. At dinner we talked about the weather or food or chores. We were all going our own ways. It wasn't so bad, just different.

The only thing I really missed was the chance to be honest with somebody. I was glad when Joanie came back and called. I went over to see her one afternoon after work. She was sitting outside her house on a lawn chair wearing a big straw hat and reading a magazine. Her face was shadowed by the wide brim of the hat. I couldn't see her nose or her eyes.

"Hi. Whatcha reading?"

She held up the magazine. I couldn't believe it.

"*Beauty Hints*?"

"It's not so bad. Where you coming from?"

"Work."

"At Marino's Beach?"

"No. The lawn job. Remember? You were there when I called up."

Very dramatically, she said, "That seems like a lifetime ago."

"It sure does."

"Actually, I never thought you'd keep that job," she said.

"How come?"

"Oh, I don't know. You're not the type."

I suddenly lost interest in telling her about the job, so I asked, "How come you're wearing that big hat?"

"I'm supposed to avoid sunburn for a while."

She took that hat off as if she was opening the curtain on a play.

She was pretty, but she wasn't Joanie. The swelling had gone down, and the bruises had disappeared. Except for the skin over the bridge of her nose, still tight and shiny, I wouldn't have been able to tell she had had a nose job. It was a good nose, I guess, but it didn't look right on that face. At least to me it didn't. Even her hair was different. She used to wear it loose, she liked it when the wind blew her hair against her face. Now it was pulled back tight in a high ponytail. So everybody could see her face.

I tried to crack a joke. "You're one of the new faces of 1952." It was the name of a Broadway show.

"You don't like it, do you?"

"When you get used to somebody..."

"The doctor said some of my friends would be very upset. They'd think..."

"I'm not very upset."

"...I was a different person. They'd have trouble talking to me..."

"I'm talking to you."

166

". . . because they had an idea of who I was, and now it would be like starting all over again. I think that's your problem."

"You must be a mind reader."

"Don't be sarcastic." She put her hat back on, which made talking to her a little easier.

"I'm not being sarcastic." I tried to be funny again. Joanie always had a great sense of humor. "I'm sure you're very attached to your new nose. Get it, attached?"

"Very funny. You ought to be on *I Love Lucy*."

"You ought to be on the *Gabriel Heatter Show*. Ah, there's good nose tonight." When she didn't make a sound, I said, "That's a joke, son."

"It's no joke, Bob. You're resentful. But I understand."

"Resentful of what?"

"Of my changing myself. The doctors said that some . . ."

"What'd you go to, a psychiatrist?"

"A plastic surgeon has to be part artist, part psychiatrist. He's a wonderful man, very kind and gentle, and he really understands people."

I was a little jealous. "How can he understand me if he never met me?"

"Because it happens all the time. You'll see, I'm still the same person."

"Except now you read *Beauty Hints* and you lost your sense of humor and you're trying to psychoanalyze me."

"That might be a good idea. Maybe you should get psychoanalyzed."

"Maybe you should have gotten your whole head chopped off."

Joanie stood up. "This is ridiculous. Come back when you're feeling like a human being." She turned her back on me and walked into the house.

I wanted to shout at her, "Come back when you look like a human being," but I couldn't.

I stopped off at Marino's Beach for a chocolate frosted and two glazed doughnuts. I wasn't even hungry. Pete was on the highboard, just jumping up and down to test the spring of the board. How could anybody do that. Up so high. I'd be afraid of slipping. But if he slipped, he'd just twist his body into a dive and plunge into the water like an arrow. But he didn't slip, he landed on the balls of his feet in the same spot on the board every time. What body control. What a body.

I bought a Three Musketeers bar for the walk up the hill. Connie counted the change twice, as if she thought I was going to cheat her out of a penny.

"Hey, big fella, how's it going?" Pete was wet. I had missed his dive.

"Okay."

"Hey." He was looking at me oddly. He circled around me. "You losing weight?"

My pants *were* feeling looser these days. "I don't know."

"Open your shirt."

"Right here?" That must have sounded silly, everybody in bathing suits, Pete just wearing his tiny trunks, his medallion and a lot of drops of water.

"C'mon." He started unbuttoning my shirt. "*Marone!* You on a diet?"

"No."

"Whatever you're doing, keep it up. Lookin' good." He slapped me on the stomach. "Next

169

thing you know, you'll be doing gainers off the highboard.''

I don't know which hurt my stomach worse, Pete's slap or the thought of going off the twenty-foot board. ''Not me.''

''Sure you will. It's the greatest feeling in the world. The moment of truth. You leave that board, big fella, and it's all up to you—you've got one second to show the world what you're made of, to show 'em you aren't afraid, to make your moves, to tell that water coming up fast, Look out, world, here comes a real man.''

''You don't have to do that to be a real man,'' I said.

''It's the best way to tell the world.'' He gave me a wink and walked back to the boats.

I didn't eat the candy bar. I ran halfway up the hill before my legs slowed down on their own. I went right into the bathroom and locked the door. I took off my clothes. I tested the bathroom scale with one toe, like Pete testing the highboard. Ready, set, go.

I stepped up on the scale, knees flexed, ready to bail out.

Numbers rolled past the pointer, up to 195,

then back down to 187. I jiggled the scale, but it always came back to 187.

I checked the dial behind the window. The needle was properly set at zero. I climbed on again.

187.

Lookin' good, big fella. I've lost at least thirteen pounds. Maybe a lot more. In one month.

I grinned at myself in the mirror. I had dimples in my cheeks. I never saw them before. I made a muscle with my right arm. It popped up. An apple of muscle pushing through the flesh. I studied the muscle. A pale blue line crossed the top of the biceps. A vein. I had a vein.

"A vein!"

My mother pounded on the bathroom door. "Bobby? Are you all right?"

"I'm fine."

"You were yelling. It sounded like the word pain."

"No, no. Rain. It looks like rain."

"It's a beautiful day. What are you doing in there?"

"I'm . . . a . . . going to the toilet."

"Do you have cramps? Are you sick?"

"I'm fine."

"When are you coming out?"

"I don't know. I'll send you a postcard."

"You're all right." She muttered and walked away.

187. And getting muscles. And veins. It was happening. I'm going to wake up thin someday.

I took a shower and dried off and examined myself in the mirror. My belly was a lot smaller. My backside didn't wobble so much. My legs looked harder. I flexed my muscles. There was no vein on my left biceps. Not yet. But there was a muscle all right. I wrapped a towel around myself and walked into my mother's room. She looked up from her desk.

"Don't drip on the floor, Bobby." She went back to her books.

I cleared my throat.

She looked up again with a false smile. "We'll eat about six, all right? If you're starving, have some fruit. There are some nice peaches and plums in the refrigerator."

"Okay." She didn't notice. She didn't really look at me. Nobody really looks at people in their own house.

I went back to my room and tried on a pair of

old shorts from two summers ago. They were snug, but I could button them. I went through all my clothes. My new summer pants were loose. The chino pants I wore four weeks ago to the carnival slid down to my hips.

On Friday, Jim Smith pulled me aside while I was sweeping the garage.

"Rumson's back in town," he said. "Better watch out."

"Maybe he better watch out." I thought I said it just right, not so tough that he'd think I was covering up feeling scared. But Jim just shook his head.

"Oh, yeah, Willie's real scared. Scared he'll kill you next time."

"We'll see." I squeezed so hard on the broom handle that my knuckles turned white. Hey. I could actually see my knuckles poking through the flesh. I never saw my knuckles before.

Jim asked, "You gonna tell him I helped you?"

"I might."

Jim made a fist. I thought he was going to slug me, but he just rubbed his mouth.

"Look, Marks, maybe I should of left you on that island."

"I would've gotten back. Willie would have brought me back."

"Okay. But I did come out to get you."

"You let him take me out there."

"What could I do?" He looked worried. "Willie's crazy. I didn't know he was going to do that."

"You're scared of him." I shouldn't have said that. Jim glared at me, but then he nodded.

"Sure I am. He's off his rocker. He'll do anything. He don't care. You know why he joined the Marines? It was that or jail. He beat up a teacher. A woman teacher."

"His uncle got him off?"

"Yeah. He's got another uncle on the school board. So they gave him a chance to straighten up and fly right."

"They ought to put him away."

"Look, I'm just telling you all this for your own good. I talked to Willie last night. I made a deal with him. If you quit this job, he'll leave you alone."

"If I don't?"

"You're on your own."

"What'll he do?"

"I don't know. He spent a couple of weeks hiding out upstate, busting his back on his brother's farm. He hates that place and he don't get along with his brother. He figures it's all your fault."

"My fault? He's crazy."

"That's what I'm trying to tell you."

"Even if I quit, Dr. Kahn wouldn't hire him anyway."

"Well, it's pretty late in the season to get anybody else, and my father would vouch for Willie. He could talk Kahn into hiring Willie. Like on a trial. And even if it doesn't work out, you'd be off the hook. Willie would figure you were even Steven. He wouldn't bother you."

"I don't know."

"He could make your life hell. Spend the rest of the summer looking over your shoulder. Scared all the time, never knowing when he's coming up behind you with a tire jack in his hand. He was talking about breaking your knee-caps last night."

"He wouldn't dare. This time he'd go to jail."

"That's what I told him. But remember, he's crazy. He don't care about nothing, he's got nothing to lose. And what's the big deal for you?

You don't really need the job. Your folks got all the money they want."

"I'll think about it."

"You better do it. Today. You quit today."

"Why do you care so much?"

"Willie's my cousin," said Jim. "I don't want to see him go down in flames over a slob like you. You do it now." He stalked away.

I was scared. Broken kneecaps. Maybe a broken head. Find me in that drainage ditch I dug. It was a lousy job anyway, killing myself for fifty cents an hour. Who needs it? Only about five more weeks till Labor Day, the end of the season. Hang around, read books, have a nice easy time. Dad's got too much on his mind to bother me anymore. Too late to go to day camp. Even if I did, it wouldn't be so horrible. Not with my new muscles. And my vein.

And Rumson really needed the job. Maybe his folks were poor. Maybe he needed something to keep from getting even crazier. Working for Dr. Kahn might help him straighten up and fly right. I'd be doing a real service, like Mom did with the charity kids. And I wouldn't really be giving up all that much.

At three o'clock I went up on the porch to collect my money. Dr. Kahn was staring at me. "What were you talking to the Smith boy about?"

"Nothing."

"I don't like a boy who lies."

"I don't even remember, it was something about trimming the bushes. He thought I should do it better."

"You're quite adequate, improving measurably. I don't want you listening to those irresponsible boys." He opened the leather purse and counted out $12.75. I had never gotten around to correcting him. Well, it doesn't matter now.

"Dr. Kahn?"

"What is it?"

"Well, uh . . ."

"Of course, how careless of me." He fished out another dollar bill. "Have a pleasant weekend." He had never said that before. He stood up. "Yes?"

"Well, uh, it's about the job."

"What about the job?" The shotgun eyes were boring into me.

You do it now. Quit. But I didn't want to. Why should I? I didn't make Willie crazy. Who says working for Dr. Kahn is going to make him sane? Dr. Kahn nearly drove me crazy. And I want a vein on my left arm, too. I'm no beach ball. No Yo-Yo. Jim Smith and his crazy cousin aren't going to jerk me up and down.

"You owe me a dollar for last week, and for the week before, too."

"That's right." He fished out two more crumpled bills. "See you Monday morning. Nine o'clock. Sharp."

The Smiths' truck was waiting for me at the bottom of the driveway. Jim leaned out. "Didja do it?"

"Nope."

"It's your funeral," he said.

His father started the truck. There. Who's a beach ball now? But I wondered: Did I really do what I wanted to do, or was I just more scared of Dr. Kahn than of Willie Rumson?

I saw Jim's face as the truck turned onto the county road. He looked worried. I was worried, too, but I didn't look it. I gave him a tight, tough smile like Humphrey Bogart in *Casablanca*.

But I was scared.

And tingling all over.

16

It's sort of interesting being scared all the time. Good experience for a writer. You wake up in the morning, feeling good, happy the sun is shining, thinking about having breakfast, then suddenly—Boom! it hits you. You've got something to be scared about. I've read stories about that. A guy wakes up, has pleasant thoughts about what's going to happen that day, then suddenly remembers he's got a terrible disease, or there's a war on, or somebody's riding into town to gun him down. Spies must feel like that. The minute you remember you're a spy—Boom! it hits you. Something to be scared about.

And then you start hearing sounds; the house creaking, footsteps in another room, a car slowing as it reaches the crest of the hill, a plane flying low. They're after me!

It's not as bad as it sounds. I mean, it's not wonderful, but it's not as if I was paralyzed with fear. Sometimes it feels good to be jittery—you really feel alive. Most of the time in my life, I always knew what was going to happen, and the only times I ever felt scared were when I thought I was going to be embarrassed. Somebody was going to make fun of my fatness in front of people I cared about. But this was a different kind of scared. Danger. Secrets. A madman out there coming after me. Willie Rumson was the hunter and I was the prey. I'd have to outsmart him.

I once read a story, it was my favorite short story for a while, called "The Most Dangerous Game" by Richard Connell. It was about a man who hunted people for sport on his own private island. One night, the hero, who was a famous hunter and writer himself, fell off a yacht and swam to that island. When he refused to hunt other men, the villain decided to hunt him. That was pretty exciting, because the hero knew all the jungle tricks. He knew how to make a Malay man-catcher and a Burmese tiger pit, and how to tie a knife to a swinging branch with vines. After a while, the hunted became the hunter. Finally, the hero beat the villain in hand-to-hand combat. I thought of myself as the hero in that story, and Willie Rumson as the villain. I'd have to outsmart him.

For starters, I never left the house without my old Cub Scout knife in one pocket and a handful of sand in the other. I imagined Willie Rumson swaggering up to me, never suspecting why I had my hands in my pockets, maybe even thinking I was gripping my legs so they wouldn't quiver from fear. Then, just as he was about to get me—Whap! I'd throw the sand right in his face. Willie would be clawing at his eyes, and I'd have a precious ten seconds to break and run, or leap on him or pull out my knife. But then the daydream got blurry. The blades stuck, they were rusty, I'd never get the knife open in time, and even if I did, then what? I don't think I could stab anybody, not even Willie Rumson out to break my kneecaps.

I kept an eye out for Rumson all that next week, especially when I walked along the county road. Ran along the county road is more like it. The only time I felt completely safe was at home with the doors locked. When I talked with Pete at Marino's Beach I felt safe because I knew that Willie was scared stiff of Pete, but I'd keep looking over my shoulder for the Chevy, knowing that as soon as I left Pete, I was on my own. I felt safe when I was mowing close to the porch with Dr. Kahn watching me like a hawk, because I knew Rumson was afraid of the old bird; but as soon as I started mowing lower down the hill toward the road, I got that jittery feeling again. It got worse the farther from the house I mowed.

But I never saw Rumson that week, and after a while I relaxed. Jim Smith might have been pulling my leg. I didn't trust him one hundred percent.

Joanie called one night and we had a friendly talk. I went to see her the next afternoon and she had cookies and lemonade waiting for me on a table on the lawn, and she was really trying to be nice.

"You look different," she said.

"I lost some weight." It was the first time I told anybody. I weighed 180 that morning.

"Are you on a diet?"

"No. It's the job."

"How much have you lost?"

"I'm not sure. Maybe twenty-five pounds."

"God, that's a lot. How do you feel?"

"Terrific."

"Not weaker?"

"I lost fat, not muscle."

"But I've heard if you lose too much weight too fast, you get weaker."

"I feel fine." Actually, I started feeling weaker just standing there listening to her.

"Not weaker in strength, but weaker in your body's ability to fight diseases. Like polio."

I was so weak I had to sit down. The word polio went into me like an ice pick.

Joanie shrugged. "I'm sure it's okay, but you have to be careful. You must really be working hard."

"It's a big lawn," I mumbled. I touched my chin to my chest. I always heard if you can touch your chin to your chest, you didn't have polio, at least not in the spine.

"How many hours a week do you work?"

"Not counting my lunch breaks, twenty-seven and a half a week."

"That's a lot of money. Twenty-seven dollars and fifty cents a week. You'll have a couple of hundred dollars by the end of the summer."

I changed the subject. I wasn't about to tell her I was getting half that much. She'd really make me feel like a rug.

"Are you up for good now?" I asked.

"I don't have to see the doctor again until September. When do you want to start working on the project?"

"Well, I don't know. I don't have a lot of time." I suddenly just wanted to get away from her.

"There isn't that much more time. Maybe you don't want to do the project anymore. It was your idea." She was trying to make me feel guilty. "If you're not interested, just let me know."

"I'm still interested. I don't have much time."

"So? I'm supposed to hang around waiting for you to have time?"

"Do you have any ideas?"

"I might." By the way her mouth snapped

shut I could tell she wasn't going to tell me what they were.

"Why don't you start without me?"

"All right, I will." It sounded like a challenge.

"I better get going, we're eating early tonight." I didn't know if we were or not.

"I'll see you," she said.

"See you."

I hit the refrigerator the minute I got back to my house. Didn't even think about it. Jerked back the metal handle, pulled open the door, let the sweet cool blast wash over my body, then plunged into the racks of food. I had one hand on a glass bowl of chocolate pudding and the other on a package of salami when a voice said, "Put it down."

"Says who?" said I.

"Says you," said Captain Marks.

"C'mon," I said, "one slice of salami isn't going to hurt, one spoonful of chocolate pudding."

"Since when," said Commander Marks, "have you ever stopped at just one of anything?"

"You eat when you feel bad," said Big Bob Marks, "and you eat when you feel good."

"Why don't you guys dry up and blow away," I said.

They all laughed.

"Listen," I said, "you guys are figments of my imagination. You know what that means?"

"It means you're stuck with us," said the Commander. "Now close the refrigerator."

I closed it.

"Keep up the good work, sir." The captain threw me a salute, and they all dried up and blew away. I went into my room to listen to the radio until dinner.

17

On Saturday Mom and I drove into the city to buy me clothes for school and bring Dad back for his two weeks' vacation. Michelle was supposed to come along, but she put up a stink; yelling, stamping her feet. It was her day off and she needed the rest, she said. She hated the city in the summertime. She wasn't going to buy any clothes till she started college and saw what the other girls were wearing. She didn't want to spend two hours each way in a hot car. Everything she said made sense to me, but from the way she carried on, even Mom must have figured out that she had something else on her mind. A big date with Pete. Sometimes Michelle isn't the world's coolest.

Mom started trying to pump me as soon as we were out of the driveway.

"I've never seen Michelle so agitated," she said.

"It *is* pretty hot in the car."

"Open your window. As soon as we're on the highway you'll get a breeze. Don't you think she knows that?"

We passed Marino's Beach. It was already crowded with families up for the weekend. Pete was on the highboard, of course. Mom nearly went off the road looking at him.

"Michelle's a very emotional person," she said. "Sometimes I think she takes after Dad more, and you take after me. We don't get so emotional about things. We kind of plug along, keep things to ourselves. Don't you think that's true?"

I didn't really think it was true, but then I hadn't ever thought about it before. So I just said, "Maybe." My mother is tricky, and I could tell she was leading up to something. I was on my guard.

"Emotional people have their ups and downs. Sometimes they do or say things they don't really mean. People like us, who really care for them, have to help them sometimes."

I wanted to say something like "Okay, Mom, lay your cards on the table," but I just said "Uh-huh."

"Bobby." She gave me a sharp glance. "You're not doing Michelle any favor by playing dumb. We're not going to be able to help her unless we're honest with each other."

"About what?"

"About what's going on."

"What's going on?"

She shook her head and didn't say another word until we were on the highway headed south toward the city. There was a breeze all right, but it was a warm breeze, and it got warmer with every mile farther from Rumson Lake.

"Maybe we should be talking about you, Bobby."

"What about me?"

"I don't like the way you've been looking. Overtired. Loss of appetite. Not your usual robust self."

"I'm getting thinner."

"That's not always a good sign. Maybe you're working too hard."

I heard warning bells in my brain, but I was trapped.

"What did you say?"

"I didn't say anything," I said.

"I'm not sure I like you hanging around Marino's Beach. It's a rough crowd."

"Mostly families." I picked my words very carefully.

"And he's taking advantage of you, not paying you."

"He's okay." I could tell she didn't even want to say Pete's name.

"Do you like him?"

"Sure."

"How much does Michelle like him?"

"Why don't you ask her?"

"Look, Bobby, this is ridiculous." Her voice was sharp. "I won't stand for lying. I want straight answers. How long has Michelle been wearing that ankle chain with the heart on it?"

"I didn't even know she had one." That was true. Who looks at his sister's legs?

"What time has she been coming home at night?"

"Am I my sister's keeper?"

"I won't stand for that, Bobby." She gripped the wheel very tightly and stared straight ahead. "I'll call up Dr. Kahn and tell him you can't work for him anymore."

I suddenly felt as if someone had flushed my insides with ice water. I felt as if I had to go to the bathroom.

"You didn't think I knew?" she asked.

"I would've told you."

"Michelle told me." Her voice softened. "Michelle cares about you, Bobby. Obviously she cares about you more than you care about her. She wanted me to know what was happening with you so I could be in a position to help you."

I was all mixed up. My mind was a mud puddle. Why had Michelle told her about my job? Why hadn't she told me she told her? We had a deal. She wasn't to be trusted. Or had Mom found out some other way and was trying to trick me?

"The two nights I was in the city, Bobby. Was Michelle out late?"

"I don't know."

"Was she home before you went to sleep?"

"I don't know."

"You can hear a door opening or closing, can't you?"

"Yes."

"Well?"

This is what it must be like to be cross-examined by Perry Mason. "I didn't hear anything at all."

"So she wasn't home when you went to sleep or you would have heard her in the house. What about when you woke up? Was she there?"

"I don't know. I didn't look."

"Well, were her breakfast dishes in the sink?"

"I don't remember."

"The night I called, Sunday night. Did you really try to wake her up? Or was she out? Now you better tell me the truth, because sooner or later I'll find out for myself, and if you've lied . . ." Just letting it hang like that really scared me.

"She wasn't there."

"The night of the storm. What time did she come back?"

"Well . . ."

"The truth."

I blurted, "She was out all night, but it wasn't her fault. Pete's truck got stuck in the mud and then . . ."

"That's all I wanted to know."

Mom didn't start talking again until we crossed the bridge into the city. Her voice was more cheerful. Why not, she got what she wanted. I felt miserable.

"Why don't we get some ice cream before we start shopping?"

"I don't want any," I said.

"It'll pick up your spirits."

"I feel fine."

"Don't feel badly. You'll see. You've done Michelle a big favor."

We met my father at the clothing store. He looked hot and tired and happy to see us.

"Let's get this over fast," he said, "this place gives me a headache. I've never seen it so crowded."

We went straight to a special department in the

basement called Huskytown. That was just a polite way of saying Fat Boys' Shop. I always hated it. It was filled with fat boys and seeing them reminded me I was fat, too. We had to wait a long time for a saleman.

"Hello, hello." The salesman whipped a tape measure off his neck and wrapped it around my waist. "We got some very nice slacks, flannels, sharkskin that wears forever. Follow me."

They did have some sharp pants, a beige pair with brown saddle stitching up the sides, and charcoal-red flannel pants the color of glowing embers. I could wear them with either checked shirts or solid-color button-down shirts. And I'd be able to wear the shirts inside my pants now.

"I like 'em," said my father.

"Look at the price, Marty."

"He'll get at least a year out of them, maybe more. Now that he's lost some weight, he should have some nice-looking pants."

"He might not stay at this weight," said my mother. "He might shoot up as soon as school starts and he's not getting as much exercise."

"I'm not going to gain weight," I said.

"Nice clothes might be an incentive for him to keep his weight down," said my father.

"You could always let them out," said the salesman.

"That's right, Lenore, worse comes to worsted." I didn't think my father's joke was too funny, but I laughed because he was on my side for a change.

"But you don't have to do the sewing, Marty." She turned to the salesman. "Can you show us some corduroys? Brown, or any dark color that won't show dirt? And chinos?"

My father gave up. "Anything you say, Lenore."

I didn't pay any more attention. I just let them push me around Huskytown, picking out underwear and shirts and socks and another pair of pants, nodding yes; anything to get out of this place in a hurry, as usual.

But I'd have money of my own this year, and when school starts I'll buy a pair of pants and a button-down shirt myself.

"Well, that wasn't so bad, was it?" said my mother as we finally left. "I'm starved. How about a nice dinner before we head back?"

"Head back?" My father looked surprised. "I thought we were staying over in the city tonight."

"I want to go back. And you can have a full day on the lake tomorrow."

"Fine with me," said my father. "We'll have to stop at the apartment to get my bags. We won't get up to Rumson Lake much before midnight. So let's eat dinner on the road, take less time."

My mother agreed too easily. She hated highway restaurants. But she really wanted to get up there tonight. I wondered about Michelle. She thought we were coming back on Sunday. If she stayed out tonight I hoped she was smart enough to fix it up with a girlfriend who would say she slept over at her house.

I dozed in the backseat with the packages on the ride up. My parents talked low. I caught snatches of their conversation.

"I'm willing to give it a try," said my father. "But I have a right to my opinion."

"Not if you're going to throw up obstacles."

"Name one."

"That business with Bobby's pants. I'm the one who has to keep them clean, and keep letting them out. If I'm working I'll have less time for things like that.''

"Then maybe you should think twice about working.''

"Let's let it drop,'' she said.

We stopped for dinner at Belle's Diner. When he pulled into the parking lot, my mother asked, "Why here?''

He pointed at a line of parked trucks. "Drivers know good food.''

"Probably just a pretty waitress,'' she said.

The food wasn't so hot, and none of the waitresses looked pretty to me. The truck drivers all sat in a row at the counter. I wondered if they sat in the same order as their trucks were parked outside. They smoked and kidded around a lot, and slapped each other's shoulders. Big, tough men. Would I ever be as cool as they are?

"Would you like a piece of cake?''

Before I could answer my mother, my father said, "Don't tempt him, Lenore. He's doing very nicely.''

"He's been such a good boy all day, a little piece of cake won't hurt him.''

"You've been pushing food into him for years, now leave him alone."

"Don't take it out on him," my mother said.

"Don't take what out?"

"Any anger at me."

"I can see this is going to be some vacation." My father got up and went to pay the check.

He drove faster than usual the rest of the way up to Rumson Lake, cutting in front of other cars, sometimes swearing at drivers who yelled at him. Once, my mother told him to take it easy.

"Bunch of road hogs out tonight," he said.

"You don't have to get us killed over a piece of cake," she said.

"What are you talking about?"

"Slow down, Marty. You're upset about what happened in the diner."

"I'm just sick and tired of all this talk, talk, talk. Do what you want. Go to work, make the kid three hundred pounds. Just leave me out of it."

"He's your son, too."

"I can't even buy him a pair of pants."

"That's different. If you're willing to take

over the care of his clothes, you can dress him any way you want."

"Let's just drop it," he said.

I tried, but I really couldn't follow the argument very well. I could see my mother's point; she really did do all the washing and ironing and sewing. But my father was willing to take a chance on getting me really nice pants for a change. He had confidence in me. And I really didn't want to eat that piece of cake. I didn't want to do anything that would make me have to go back to Huskytown.

I wondered if the argument was less about me than about my mother going to work. Sometimes grown-ups fight about one thing, when they're really thinking about something else.

It was after midnight when we got to Rumson Lake. The town was shut up except for the bars. The lake was silent and calm. There were a few cookout fires along the shore, and I could see dots of light, flashlights maybe, or campfires, on the island. I wondered if Michelle was on the island with Pete.

We turned up our hill. In the moonlight, I caught a glimpse of a white pickup truck parked among some bushes off a side road. It looked like the Marino Express. Why would Pete hide his truck near our house?

I got an answer to that pretty quick. There was a car in our driveway, its headlights blazing. Mr. Marino's maroon Cadillac. There were three figures spotlighted in the beams like actors on a stage. Mr. Marino was shaking his finger at Pete and Michelle. They were listening with their heads down.

"What the hell is this?" said my father. He was out of the car almost before he came to a full stop.

"Marty..." called my mother, but it was too late. He charged around the car. We followed right behind him.

"What's going on here?" my father shouted.

Mr. Marino whirled. "That's a good question, but a little late. Some father you are."

"What are you doing here?"

"Taking my son home."

"What's he doing here?"

"Ask that trampy daughter of yours."

My father went right for Mr. Marino's throat, arms out, his hands like claws. They were about the same height, but Mr. Marino was much heavier. He swung at my father. His punch missed, but his arm knocked my father's arm away. Both of them stumbled, then collided with a thud and grabbed each other's shoulders. They began wrestling against the side of the Cadillac.

Michelle was screaming and Pete was frozen stiff, a statue like me. It was my mother who moved first. She flew at Dad and Mr. Marino, pulled at their clothes, somehow got between them and pushed them apart.

"Michelle! Into the house!" shouted my mother. "Bobby! Into the house!"

I followed Michelle up the gravel path. She stopped at the front steps to bury her face in her hands and sob. I wanted to put my arm around her shoulder, she seemed so shrunken up, but I had never done it before and I didn't know how. I patted her arm, and she reached out and hugged me and cried on my shoulder. It was a strange feeling, but not bad.

After a while, we went inside and looked out the window. We couldn't hear what they were saying in the driveway, but from the way Mr. Marino smacked his fist into his palm and my father leaned toward him like a cobra about to strike, I figured it wasn't friendly. Pete was sitting in the front seat of his father's car. My mother was talking to him through the open passenger window, but he didn't seem to be talking back, just nodding or shaking his head or shrugging.

"I thought you were coming back tomorrow," said Michelle. She had stopped crying, but she kept wiping her nose.

"Mom changed her mind. What happened?"

"He caught us here. Pete's father." She started crying again. I gave her a piece of Kleenex I found in my pocket.

"You should have gone to the island," I said.

"Pete wouldn't go. He doesn't think it's . . . right."

The argument in the driveway didn't seem to end so much as just run down, like a windup toy. After a while, Mr. Marino wasn't pounding his fist so often, and my father's body relaxed, and their mouths weren't moving so fast. They began waving at each other, as if they were brushing away flies, and I could imagine them saying things like "Don't give me that," or "Get off it,'' or ''Why don't you just dry up and blow away.''

Finally, Mr. Marino got into his car and raced the motor until my father got into his car and pulled out of the driveway so Mr. Marino could back out.

''They're coming in now,'' I told Michelle.

''All of them?''

''Just Mom and Dad.''

''Stay with me?''

''You betchum, Red Ryder.'' I felt very protective toward her. It was a good feeling, it made me feel older and stronger, but it only lasted a couple of minutes. The first thing Dad said when he got into the house was ''Robert. To bed. This instant.''

Mom took Michelle in her arms, and Dad stood there glaring at them, tapping his foot. That was the end of the show for me. I kept my ear at the open crack of my door, but I didn't hear another word that night.

18

I made myself invisible for a while. Like The Shadow. An old trick I picked up as a kid. Adults just want to know you're alive and healthy. So if you go about your business quietly, eat your meals, smile and always look like you've got something to do that will keep you out of trouble, nobody notices you much. I stayed out of everybody's way, didn't spend too much time on the toilet, and hardly ever spoke unless Mom or Dad spoke first. And they were so busy with themselves and with Michelle, they hardly talked to me for three or four days, and then mostly to remind me to wash my hands for dinner.

I went to work and came right home, trotting along the county road looking over my shoulder for Rumson's Chevy. I steered clear of Marino's

Beach. I didn't call Joanie. And every evening after dinner I weighed myself. That's the heaviest time. When I got down to 176 I danced around the bathroom and popped muscles in the mirror till they were sore. Wunderbar. I knew I'd be under 175 when I woke up. Another fifteen pounds and I'd be thin. Well, maybe not thin, but nobody would ever call me fat.

I took off my shirt one afternoon at Dr. Kahn's. That was a big thing. I hadn't walked around with my shirt off since I was little. Flesh still hung over my belt, but I felt like Charles Atlas compared to what I used to be. A 196-pound weakling.

Michelle and I didn't talk until the middle of the week. Her eyes were red for days, she couldn't look at anybody, and right after dinner she would go straight to her room and listen to her Johnny Ray records. All those dumb songs about crying. I felt sorry for her, but enough was enough. She might drown in her room if she kept playing those songs.

One night I was in my bed reading *The Book of Woodcraft* by Ernest Thompson Seton, just in case I got trapped on the island again, when Michelle walked in without knocking.

"Just one question, Bobby? Why did you tell her I was out all night?"

"Why did you tell her about my job? We had a deal."

She sat down on my bed. "Did she say you would be helping me? That if you really cared about me you'd tell her the truth?"

"How'd you know?"

"Because that's why I told her about your job." She leaned over and kissed my forehead. "It's okay. Don't worry about it."

"Are you ever going to see Pete again?"

"Of course."

"How?"

"We'll find a way."

"Next month you'll be in the dorms, you'll do whatever you want," I said.

"You better believe it." She smiled for the first time in days.

I had a dream that night. I was standing on the highboard. There was no water below me, just a net, the kind they use in the circus for trapeze artists. Everybody was yelling for me to jump—

Dr. Kahn, Mom and Dad, Pete, Michelle, Willie Rumson, Jim Smith, Mr. Marino, even the man from the grocery store. I was scared, I didn't want to jump, but they kept screaming for me to jump, to show I was a man; if I didn't jump I couldn't be a man, I'd be a fag all my life. A rug, a beach ball, a Yo-Yo. But I couldn't jump. I was too scared. I turned around to walk back to the platform, but Joanie blocked my way. She was walking out toward me on the board. It didn't really look like Joanie, even with her new nose; she was taller and older and her hair was darker, but somehow I knew it was Joanie. She was wearing a two-piece bathing suit and she had a bigger bosom than Joanie, but I knew it was her. And then she threw her arms around me and squeezed me tight, and suddenly I felt hot and wet, that good, exciting feeling, and then she shoved me off the board. As I fell, I saw they had dragged the net away, and I was just falling, falling, falling . . .

Naturally, I woke up before I hit anything. You always do.

I have dreams like that every so often. I've tried to look them up in a book we have about dreams by Sigmund Freud, but all I can figure out is that they have something to do with sex. I really wanted to talk to somebody about it. But Michelle was busy crying and Mom was busy studying and Joanie would have looked down her nose at me. That's a joke, son. I might have tried Dad, he was so quiet and pleasant these days, but he was hardly ever around. He really knew how to make himself invisible. He just disappeared for hours and hours at a time. Tennis, swimming, softball games, golf, going to the lumberyard for special kinds of wood, working in the basement with his carpentry tools, going up on the roof to replace broken shingles. I could tell he just didn't want to talk to anybody. I know he knew about my lawn job, because he asked me one morning if I was using his work gloves, and when I said I was, he said he'd get himself another pair. And that was it. He didn't ask me any questions at all.

That Friday, Jim Smith came up to me and looked me in the eye for a few seconds and said, "Buddy, you're either crazy or you got the guts of a burglar."

"What do you mean?"

"You're still here. Look, this is the last time I'm gonna say anything to you. Willie's been drinking all week, he's really getting himself mean. Nobody'll go near him. He's gonna come after you like gangbusters."

"You told me that already. And nothing happened."

"Look, you got three lousy weeks left on this job. Nothin'. Quit. You do that and I'll try to head him off."

I got the feeling Jim was begging me, not warning me. I just shook my head.

But I kept my eyes peeled for Rumson the rest of the afternoon, and when I trotted home on the county road I did zigzags, just in case he was hiding somewhere in ambush, ready to run me down. Drivers must have thought I was crazy.

I wasn't crazy at all. I was rounding the last bend before Marino's Beach when I saw the blue-and-white Chevy coming fast in the other direction. I ducked behind an old stone farm wall. The Chevy passed without slowing down. I tracked it around the lake. It turned up to Dr. Kahn's.

I had to make a decision. I could run for it, all

the way home, and take a chance on getting trapped on the road or on the hill. Or I could go into Marino's Beach and play it by ear from there. If Willie was really hunting me, once he found I wasn't at Dr. Kahn's, he'd come back down the road, slowly. If he wasn't hunting me, he might just be on his way to Lenape Falls, and I'd be standing around Marino's Beach, trying to avoid Pete. I was still trying to figure out my next move when I saw the Chevy come tearing out on the county road. I ran all the way to Marino's Beach.

"Bob!" It was Joanie. She was behind the snack bar counter.

When I caught my breath, I said, "What are you doing here?"

"Working." She really looked different now. A big red bow on her ponytail. Lipstick. A red bathing suit with white polka dots. *Beauty Hints*. She still didn't resemble the girl in my dream, but she was a lot closer. "Like a Coke?"

"Sure."

She looked like she knew what she was doing. She pulled a frosty bottle out of the big red Coca-Cola chest, popped off the cap with one flick of her wrist, and dropped a yellow straw into the bottle. "Here you go." She banged the bottle down in front of me like a bartender in a western movie. "On the house."

"How long have you been working here?"

"Since Wednesday."

"How'd you get the job?"

"I came down to talk to Pete and Connie about the project..."

"Our project?"

"I thought I'd write something about small businesses. For Economics." She arched her eyebrows. I never saw that before. She must have practiced in the mirror. "Pete was too busy to talk because Connie was sick, so I helped out. I did such a good job he's giving me fifty cents an hour. It isn't very much, but I get lunch, and tips."

"That's great."

"Don't get carried away now."

"No, I really mean it. Are you going to work the rest of the summer?"

"I don't know. Connie should be back soon, but Pete thinks I'm terrific, so..." She tossed her ponytail. Another new gesture. I wondered if there was a special department for gestures in *Beauty Hints*. Or had the plastic surgeon given her a list of new moves to go with her new nose.

"Do you like the job?"

"It's fabulous. I'm meeting a lot of people." Just the way she said it, I knew she meant boys. "What's new?"

"Nothing much."

She leaned over the counter. "I heard Pete and Michelle broke up."

"Yeah."

"What happened?"

"Ask them."

"C'mon, you can tell *me*."

Whoever *you* are, I thought. I felt I was talking to a stranger.

"There's that creep again," she said.

I turned in time to see Willie Rumson's face framed in his car window. He passed slowly, giving me the once-over. It sent chills up my spine.

"You know him?" I asked coolly.

"Seen him around. Don't you remember, he was one of those hoods at the carnival? He's been cruising up and down the road all week. He stopped once and asked me for a date." She made a face, but I could tell she was a little bit proud.

"What'd you say?"

"I told him I don't go out with strangers."

"Have you...uh...been...you know, going out?"

"I might. There's another guy who's been hanging around the last few days. He's going to college next year." She tossed her ponytail again. She was turning into a real tease. Probably try out for cheerleaders when we go back to school. "Pete doesn't like him too much."

I was really getting tired of her. "Why don't you go make out with Pete?"

"Hmmmmmm." She pretended she was considering it. "Hey, what's the story about Pete and Michelle? What happened?"

"Don't you remember, curiosity killed the cat?"

"But satisfaction...there he is again."

Willie Rumson was cruising past again, really casing the joint. When he caught me staring at him, he hit the accelerator and burned rubber down the road.

I looked around. Marino's Beach was emptying out. The sky was overcast and the air was cool. It wasn't a good swimming or sunbathing day. And summer people go home early on Friday afternoons to make dinner for the men coming up for the weekend. There were just a few families left on the sand, and a couple of kids jumping off the diving boards. Pete was tying up the boats.

"How do you get home?" I asked Joanie.

"Sometimes I walk, but Pete said he'd drive me back today. You want a lift?"

"I think so."

"Are you nervous about something?"

"Can I have another Coke?"

"You'll have to pay for this one."

"Okay."

She got it for me and started wiping down the counter. "Excuse me, I've got to clean up now."

I looked for Rumson on the road. There was a lot of traffic now, and I might have missed him. Maybe he just gave up and drove away. I could still make a run for it; with all the cars on the county road he probably wouldn't try anything.

But if he was as crazy as Jim Smith said, he just might not care.

The kids on the diving boards were called in by their mothers. There were only two families on the beach, and they were packing to leave. Pete had finished tying up the boats and was raking the sand. He'd be closing in a few minutes. I didn't want to face him, but it was better than facing Willie Rumson.

It was getting chillier. It might rain tonight. The sun disappeared behind a gray cloud. It felt like a fall day. Fall was in the air. Then school. If I lived that long.

I thought I saw a blue-and-white car turn up a driveway a few hundred yards up the road. Rumson? Just waiting?

"Da dum," said Joanie. "How's it look?" She waved toward the neat rows of candies and packaged cakes and paper cups. The faucets and the milk shake machine and the hot dog griddle gleamed.

"Gorgeous," I said.

Pete walked up carrying the rake and a bag of trash. When he saw me he started to turn away.

"Pete," said Joanie, "could you give Bob a lift home?"

"No, sorry," he mumbled, and went behind the shack.

The last two families got in their cars and drove away. The beach was empty. Except for the Marino Express, the parking lot was empty. In the distance, I heard thunder. Or was it Willie Rumson revving up his car?

I found a nickel and called home. Mom and Dad or Michelle would pick me up.

The line was busy.

I panicked and ran around to the back of the shack. Pete was locking up the first-aid room.

"Willie Rumson's after me," I said.

"He's nothing."

"Maybe to you. But I can't take him. And he might have a knife or a tire jack."

"Don't worry about it." He wouldn't look at me. "He's all bluff."

"I've been calling his bluff all summer and he keeps beating me up. Jim Smith said..."

"Another Rummie punk."

"Could you drive me halfway up the hill?"

Pete finally looked at me. His face was twisted.

"I'm not allowed. I promised my father. I'm not even supposed to talk to you."

"To me?"

"To any member of your family."

"Aren't you ever going to call up Michelle?"

He turned his back on me.

I ran back to the telephone. The line was still busy. It could be Michelle talking to a girlfriend. Every so often she gets into a marathon, and this could be one of them.

"What's the matter, Bob?" asked Joanie.

"Pete won't drive me home."

"C'mon, I'll talk to him."

We walked around the shack. Pete was rearranging some tools in the storage shed. I realized he'd been stalling around till I went away.

"Pete," said Joanie, "why can't you . . ."

Pete was looking over her shoulder, his mouth open. We turned to see Willie Rumson swaggering toward us with a .22 rifle in his hand.

19

"Just turn around and go out on the dock," said Rumson. He was swaying from side to side.

"Put that down," said Pete, "or I'll shove it down your throat."

Rumson raised the rifle and pointed it at Pete's medallion. "Out in the dock."

"You don't have the guts to use that, Rummie," said Pete. I hoped Pete knew what he was doing. But I wasn't so sure.

Rumson raised the rifle to his shoulder. I remembered him at the carnival, right here, puncturing balloons with a BB gun faster than Vinnie Marino could blow them up.

"He's a crack shot," I said.

"He's a yellow-bellied coward," said Pete. He took a step forward.

I imagined Willie's finger tightening on the trigger.

Joanie jumped in front of Pete and turned him around. She pushed him toward the dock. I was surprised at how easily such a small girl could move such a big, powerful guy.

"You, too, beach ball," said Willie.

We walked out on the dock. No one could see us from the road now, the snack bar blocked the view. The sand beaches alongside Marino's were empty, too. There weren't even any boats on the lake. Maybe someone across the lake or on the island watching through binoculars could see us, but they'd just see four people standing on a dock, one of them with a stick in his hand. Even if they could make out the rifle, they wouldn't call the police. Plenty of people had rifles on Rumson Lake.

"What are you going to do?" asked Joanie.

"Just let a little air out of the beach ball," said Rumson. "One knee, that's all."

"Dumb Rummie," said Pete. "Before you crank that bolt for a second shot I'll be standing on your face. There won't be enough of you left to put in jail."

Willie laughed. "I'll blow a hole in the fat boy and one in you before you can say Hail Mary, guinea." He held the rifle in one hand as if it were a long pistol. It wasn't too steady. He might miss my knee, but he'd hit something. Like my stomach or my heart.

"Just put that down."

I wondered if Pete was stalling for time. Waiting for something to happen. I'd seen it a hundred times before in movies, and done it myself in daydreams. But what could happen here? The U.S. Cavalry? A bolt of lightning? Superman?

"Untie one of those rowboats," said Willie to Joanie.

"Don't do it," said Pete.

"I'll give her an extra hole if she don't," said Willie.

"He's bluffing," said Pete.

Joanie looked from Pete to Willie. She didn't know what to do.

I asked, "Where you going to take us?" I didn't want to make Willie any crazier, so I made my voice sound scared. It wasn't hard.

"Back to the island," said Willie. "Finish off what I started, fat boy."

My mind raced. In the rowboat or even on the island we might have a better chance than standing here on the dock. Tip the boat getting in or out, snap a branch back in Willie's face on the island. I had some ideas.

"Untie the boat," I told Joanie.

"Don't do it," said Pete.

She looked from Pete to Willie to me, trying to make up her mind.

"Hey, Willie." Jim Smith ambled out on the dock. Slow and easy, his hands in the pockets of his rust-colored pegged pants. He was wearing blue-suede shoes and a sky-blue shirt with a rolled collar. I never saw him dressed up before.

"What the hell you want, Jimmy?"

"C'mon, let's go up to Lenape. I got a couple chicks lined up. Hot to trot. Yours got knockers you won't believe."

"Leave me alone."

"You did it, Willie, you scared the crap out of them. They couldn't spit if their feet were on fire. So let's go and have some real fun."

"I'm gonna shoot the fat boy in the knee. And maybe the guinea, too."

"They're not worth the slugs, Willie."

"You gotta take a stand somewhere." That vein started pumping on Willie's forehead. "No guts around here. Let 'em walk all over us. You hear they want to change the name of the lake? They stole it and now they want to take the name away, too."

"That's just talk, Willie." Jim's voice was soft, as if he were talking to a child.

But Rumson's voice was getting louder. "They'll do it, they'll do it, call it Kike Lake or Wop Lake, maybe Nigger Lake, but I'm gonna stop it, stop it right now, my Pa didn't have the guts and look at your Pa, gonna have to work till he drops dead, too, this used to be our lake, now I can't even get a lousy job cutting some Jew's grass."

"You're not gonna get a job this way."

"Ain't for me, it's for all of us, I don't care what happens to me," he was screaming now, "but they ain't gonna push Rumsons around no more, this'll be a warning to all of them."

He aimed the rifle at my chest.

Jim yelled, "Go ahead and kill 'im, Willie, go ahead, you brought enough grief to your Ma, might as well really fix her good this time, give her a stroke, too."

"Huh?" The rifle wavered.

"Go ahead, dig her grave a little deeper, wasn't enough you couldn't finish school, got yourself kicked out of the Marines, wrecked those cars, never brought no money into the house, go ahead and kill your Ma, too."

"Don't say that, Jimmy." He whirled and pointed the rifle at Jim.

"Yeah, and while you're at it, kill her sister's boy, too." Jim walked right into the rifle until the tip of the barrel was against his shirt.

"Jimmy." It was like a baby's moan.

Smith snatched the rifle out of Willie's hands, and put his arm around Willie's shoulders. "C'mon, Willie, let's get out of here. I'll take you home with me."

They started to walk away, Willie leaning against Jim. My knees felt weak. I looked at Joanie. There were tears in her eyes. I turned to look at Pete. He was poised to spring, as if he was about to go off the highboard.

Joanie shrieked, "No."

Pete was a brown blur moving fast. Three long strides up the dock, a giant leap and he was crashing down on the backs of Smith and Rumson.

There was a solid thunk, and the three of them were in a heap on the dock. Jim Smith rolled away. Pete grabbed Rumson by the throat and lifted him into the air.

Jim got up slowly, shaking his head to clear it. He picked up the rifle. There was a loud clack as he snapped the bolt home. The sound stopped Pete cold. He lowered Rumson.

"He didn't even have a slug in the chamber," said Jim. Blood was running out of both nostrils. "But there's one in there now. Let him go."

Pete's hands opened on Rumson's throat. Willie rubbed his neck. His eyes were wide, he was breathing fast. That vein was pumping so hard I was sure it would burst through the skin of his forehead.

"You musclebound ass," said Jim. "Why'd you have to do that?"

"Nobody pushes me around," said Pete.

"No, you're a real man, a regular John Wayne, just like Willie."

Willie was looking around wildly, from Jim to Pete to Joanie to me, before something seemed to click in his mind. He put his head down and charged at me.

I saw him coming in slow motion. I heard Joanie and Pete yell. But I couldn't move, couldn't even think fast enough to brace my feet, just watched his head slam into my chest, and then the two of us were rolling around on the dock, holding each other.

I squeezed as hard as I could and heard him gasp, but his arms were free and his fists pounded my back and kidneys and my neck and my head. I was dizzy, there was a ringing in my ears and I felt the strength draining out of my arms. In a few seconds he'd break free, and then those combat boots would be stomping my face.

I used the last of my strength to roll us toward the edge of the dock. I was heavier and I could move his body.

We rolled off the dock locked together.

Just before we hit the water I took a deep breath and held it. As we sank I wrapped my legs around his waist and my arms around his head. We went down. He struggled in my grip. He reached up to pull my hair and claw my face, to climb back up to air.

But I had him. I had him good and tight. Under water. My territory.

I felt a surge of triumph as his struggling grew weaker. You finally messed with me in the wrong place, Willie-boy. I'm the underwater champ. I spent my whole life waiting for a punk like you, I spent my whole life underwater, hiding out so no one could see me. You should have shot me while you had the chance.

I felt him go limp and I still had breath, keep him down another couple of seconds in case he's faking, but then strong arms separated us, and someone was pushing me up, and I shot to the surface. The air was delicious in my burning lungs. Jim was in the water, pushing Willie up the ladder ahead of him. I climbed up after them.

Willie collapsed on the dock. His skinny body shook and heaved. His fingers clawed at the wet wood. He tried to raise his head but couldn't. He vomited. His legs twitched. He gulped air and choked on it. I felt sick.

Jim kneeled beside him, rubbing Willie's back, holding his forehead while he retched.

"Okay," said Pete. "Get that punk on his feet."

Pete had the rifle.

"Leave him alone," said Jim.

"He's going to jail, and if you don't move your tail you're going, too. Get him up."

Jim took his time, stroking Willie, soothing him. Then, very slowly, he lifted Willie to his feet and hoisted him over his shoulders in a fireman's carry. Jim started up the dock toward his pickup truck, staggering under Willie's body.

"Hold it right there," boomed Pete.

Jim Smith turned. "You're worse than he is, Tarzan." He stared at Pete with disgust. Then he turned away and walked out of Marino's Beach and never looked back.

Pete lowered the rifle. Joanie whispered, "Oh, God." We watched Jim load Willie into the cab of his truck. Willie was retching out the window as the truck pulled away.

When the truck was out of sight, Pete said, "Well, we did it. Open up the snack bar, Joanie, break out some Cokes."

"I don't feel like anything now," said Joanie in a weak voice. "I'd like to go home."

"I'll drive you." Pete grinned at me. "Both of you."

"Thanks anyway," I said. "I'll walk."

"I'll take you all the way up the hill, big fella.

You deserve it.'' He threw an arm over my shoulder. I was too tired to push it off, but I wanted to.

"That's okay."

"I insist. You really gave that punk something he'll remember the rest of his life. You're a hero."

I walked out from under his arm. "Why'd you have to do it, Pete?"

"Do what?" He didn't know what I was talking about.

"Jump them. After it was all over."

"Are you serious? Let 'em get away with that? Push us around like that?"

I left him standing there, the rifle in his hand, shaking his head. He would never understand what I was talking about.

Halfway up my hill I had to catch my pants before they slipped off my waist. The Cub Scout knife and the handful of wet sand in my pockets were dragging them down. I had completely forgotten about my secret weapons. Some hero.

20

There were little white tables with striped umbrellas on Dr. Kahn's lawn, and workmen were erecting a huge tent in front of the house. Dr. Kahn was standing at the top of the porch steps directing them. I stood for five minutes at the bottom of the porch steps before he looked down at me.

"Today is Saturday," he said.

I wanted to answer, like Bogie would, "I'm a little early, Doc," but I was too nervous. And I didn't want to be wise with him.

"Could I talk to you a minute?"

"One minute. Can't you see I've very busy? My nephew's getting married here tomorrow."

"It's about the job. I don't think fifty cents an hour is fair."

"You agreed to it."

"Well, that was because I was so slow in the beginning. But I've improved. I do the lawn in two days now. The place really looks beautiful, doesn't it?"

"I don't like a boy who reneges on a deal."

"I want a dollar an hour. Just like you said in the beginning of the summer."

"I never said it."

"It was on the card on the bulletin board when I called. A dollar an hour."

He stared at me. Just like he did the very first time, a lifetime ago. But those shotgun eyes didn't scare me anymore.

"You should pay me for this summer," said Dr. Kahn. "I've watched you change from a miserable fat boy into a fairly presentable young man. On my lawn. On my time."

"You didn't do it, Dr. Kahn. I did it."

His thin lips twitched. I wondered if he was finally going to smile. He didn't. After a long time, he said, "Starting Monday, for the remainder of the season, one dollar an hour. But you'll have to prove to me you are worth every penny of this generous raise. Nine o'clock. Sharp.'' He turned back to the tent. I was dismissed.

I skipped down the gravel driveway. I jogged along the county road. I didn't have to look over my shoulder. Nothing's behind me now, everything's up ahead.

I got to Marino's Beach before I realized I had walked that far. Not even breathing hard. The beach was crowded. Families were spread out along the sandy shore. Kids were screaming and diving and splashing each other in the sparkling water. Sailboats and rowboats danced on the lake.

Pete was standing on the highboard, as usual, surveying his kingdom. The One and Only. Pe the Great. Everything I wanted to be when the summer started. I imagined him going off the highboard, turning in the air, knifing into the water. I remembered him telling me about being a man. You leave the board, big fella, and it's all up to you, you've got one second to show the world what you're made of, to show 'em you aren't afraid, to make your moves, to tell that water coming up fast, Look out, world, here comes a man.

Pete didn't know any more about being a man than I did. Or Willie Rumson. I thought of Willie on the dock, retching his guts out. I might have drowned him. Because of Pete. Poor Willie, just a crazy mixed-up guy who couldn't do anything right and tried to make himself feel better by deciding all his problems were caused by the only kid around he was sure he could take. And he couldn't even take him.

Pete went off the board, hit the water, and surfaced to applause from some girls on the dock. Someday I might go off that highboard. Maybe even this summer. And maybe not. Who knows? Three more weeks till Labor Day, a lot could happen. Summer isn't over yet. I like summer. All the seasons are terrific.

Also by Robert Lipsyte

Pb 0-06-447039-3   Pb 0-06-447079-2   Pb 0-06-447097-0   Hc 0-06-000496-7
                                                          Pb 0-06-000498-3

The Contender
Alfred's a kid with no direction and no future—until he starts training at a famous Harlem boxing club and learns that it's the work, not the win, that makes the man.

The Brave
Sonny Bear's been an outsider all his life. On the Reservation, they see him as white. Whites call him Indian. Sonny leaves for New York, but he doesn't count on tangling with a tough boxer turned cop named Alfred Brooks. Alfred thinks Sonny can make it to the top, be a contender, if he can take control and beat the anger inside him.

The Chief
Sonny Bear has a championship left hook but his career's going nowhere. He's almost ready to hang it up when his manager, Alfred Brooks, schemes him into a glitzy Vegas match. Suddenly Sonny's headed for stardom. But sometimes fame isn't all it's cracked up to be.

Warrior Angel
Sonny Bear is on a fast track to defeat. Nothing matters to him—not even the title. Then he meets Starkey, a mysterious kid who is sure he can get Sonny back in the ring. But will Sonny's rise to the top mean a knockout for Starkey?

www.harperchildrens.com   ⬛HarperTrophy®
An Imprint of HarperCollinsPublishers